THE VESPER FILE

BOOK 3 IN THE ERIN REED TRILOGY

A.J. FONTENOT

THE VESPER FILE

"I was born for the storm, and a calm does not suit me."

— ANDREW JACKSON (1767-1845)

A NOTE

The word *vesper* is Latin for "evening star," a forerunner of the coming darkness. And some liturgical branches of Christianity use the same name for their last prayer.

PREVIOUSLY

THE CENTURY MAN LEFT OFF WITH BEN, STILL IN Colombia, reeling from the events that had just happened. Meanwhile, Erin was boarding a plane to Tangier, Morocco, to investigate Paul's cryptic message.

But it's not long before she realizes the new lead she has is just the tip of the iceberg. The more she learns, the more questions she has…

The Vesper File — the final installment in the Erin Reed trilogy — picks up one week later…

2

COLLECT AND KILL

"Valentina," Eli Bren said. "This a secure line?"

His voice was silky. Like he was happy. Like he'd just done something.

"Yes," she said.

"Good, good."

She could hear noises in the background.

"I just landed in D.C.," he said. "And...," he said, drawing the word out. "We have the location."

"Where?" she said.

"Tangier."

"Where?"

"Morocco. The southern half of the Straight of Gibraltar."

"And the package is there?" she said.

"Yes," he said.

"And, what about the girl?"

"Same."

Val was still in Colombia. After they'd left, they each went their separate ways. Eli to one of his properties some-where else. Jonah to...who knows where. And Val, she stayed in Colombia. She'd been…tying up a few loose ends. Doing the work that would make sure no one followed them forward.

"I'll leave now. For Tangier," Val said.

"No," Eli said. "I have something else I want you to do. I need you here, in D.C. Send someone else to Tangier. But, Valentina, choose them well. Expense is not an issue. Accuracy is."

"Collect and kill?" she said.

Eli was quiet for a long moment.

"Eli?" she said.

"Collect first," he said. "The package is the top priority. Capture is *not* an option."

'Not an option' is an industry term that meant: if captured, the client will hire another operator to come and eliminate you.

"And kill?" Val asked.

"If necessary," he said.

"That's a kill for *anyone* who gets in the way?" Val said. She knew what this meant. What it meant to Eli. Even if he didn't know she knew.

"Yes," Eli said, ending the call.

Val thumbed through her contacts and dialed the first of a several calls she'd need to make.

TANGIER, MOROCCO

Erin sat, reading the same word over and over.

And then the sentences around it.

And then the page.

Father.

She needed more information. And Paul's notes were written so matter-of-factly, as if there wasn't a question in his mind when he'd written them.

Did that really mean...? she wondered. No... it couldn't...

She pushed her chair back and stood up. She'd been sitting in this dusty underground room for the better part of four hours. Sabeer had left some time back. He had other business, he told her. Which was fine, because she had enough to do here. Paul had stockpiled copious notes of a dozen major investigations and countless related details. From what she could tell, his notes spanned a good quarter of a century, to right around the time Gillian was killed.

Up to this point, Erin had been on a tear. Completely engrossed in what she was uncovering.

She stood up, she realized she hadn't moved for at least two hours. She lifted her hands above her head, stretching. While here, delving into Paul's secret storeroom in Sabeer's basement in Morocco, she'd uncovered the evidence she needed to put Eli Bren away for good. And, in some parts, if not the exact evidence, Paul had detailed the chain of knowledge connecting it all. The dots were all here. And most of them Paul had connected over the years. Some of what was here were duplicates of classified reports. *Highly* classified stuff. And, by the looks of it, some of this stuff Paul wasn't supposed to have known about.

She understood now why he didn't share this before. Not only was it damning. It was dangerous.

But then she'd found something she didn't expect. Something that blindsided her.

She'd regularly seen threads about Gillian, her mother. Some were dead ends. Others were stories she was familiar with. And others still were theories or intel that were completely new to Erin.

And it was in one of these reports that Erin came across her own name.

But it wasn't seeing her name that stopped her. It was the context.

Paul had just named Erin's father.

Erin's father.

All the theories she'd developed when she was younger. The search in college to find him. All of it... she was not even remotely close.

And now, the man's name Erin was reading in Paul's notes was making her head spin. Because she knew him.

She sat back down at the dusty desk again. She pulled a stack she'd previously skimmed through. She'd go back to the genesis of this particular story. Putting the pieces together, one by one. Paul had to have missed something. And whatever assumptions he was basing this on, she'd find them, and then figure out what this was really all about.

She'd start from the beginning. Follow the threads. At the very least she needed to understand why Paul would have—

"Erin," came a voice from the low cut door leading into this room.

Sabeer ducked his head as he walked in.

The room was essentially a locked vault. It was underground, below Sabeer's shop in the old part of Tangier. In the back of his shop, a false floor opened to a storeroom. That storeroom had *another* hidden door inside it. And behind that door was a winding tunnel, stretching about forty feet or so. The tunnel ended at a small wooden door, with a room and some old equipment. Then, inside *that* room was a steel door. And for the last quarter of a century, Paul had kept that steel door locked from every other person. That was, until Paul sent that last message to Ben and Sabeer. Ben's message was a cryptic "start Vesper" and Sabeer's message was the code to open this room.

And — what she didn't know at the time, because her phone had died — was that Paul had sent her a message too. Her message had two international phone numbers. Or, that's what she initially thought until she realized they were GPS coordinates. Of Sabeer's shop, as it turned out.

In his last living act, Paul had officially turned over the keys to the investigation he'd spent the last twenty-five years building. An investigation, that when given the right platform, would right more than a few wrongs.

"Erin," Sabeer said again. But he was whispering.

Something was wrong. His expression was tense.

She looked up at him. "What," she said, taking a deep breath, pulling her thoughts back to the present. "What's wrong…"

"Shhh," he said, holding up a hand. He was carrying his cell phone in his other hand. He showed it to her, carefully, as if it might explode if he shook it.

"I don't under—" she whispered back to him.

"Someone's here," he mouthed.

4

JONAH LENNOX

A FEW MINUTES AGO, JONAH LENNOX HAD BEEN SITTING in a small bistro on a small busy street in downtown Tangier. He was dressed in white and tan linen. And, if it weren't for his light blonde hair, he might actually blend in. Well, that *and* the fact that he was carrying a Ruger SR22 pistol in his jacket under his left armpit.

Jonah wasn't normally the type for guns. Not that he couldn't use them. Growing up, the kinds of schools Eli sent him away to generally had blue-blood sports like archery and rifle. And, to his credit, he'd become quite good. But in the real world, guns lacked finesse. Any idiot could pick one up and become dangerous. There was no challenge. Nothing to earn. Only a kind of brute force. A poorly disguised weakness.

But... then again, desperate times called for desperate measures.

He'd been following his mark from a distance. And he wasn't a hard man to follow. So far, he'd made no effort to double-back or check over his shoulder or any of the usual signs of paranoia. From the looks of it, he still had no idea he was being followed.

Jonah felt the weight of the silencer in his jacket pocket sway as he walked on.

The streets were busy. He slowed his pace.

The man walked into an outdoor market. Jonah followed. As he did, he gave his mark enough distance to get ahead. Jonah stopped next to a merchant's stall, where a woman stood against racks of hand made things. She pulled one off the rack and put it in front of his face. Jonah shewed her away, keeping his eyes on the mark the whole time.

The man walked out the back of the market, and Jonah followed. He moved down a small alley, crossing to another street, just as busy as the one he'd come from. He walked like he knew exactly where he was going. Like a local who frequented this route. And he would certainly *be* a local… for this kind of job.

Across the street, Jonah stopped and watched.

The man walked into a small tea shop. The words above the entrance were written in Arabic and another boxy language Jonah didn't recognize.

Jonah moved to cross the street. He stood on the outside of the shop, next to the entrance. The noise from the street made it impossible to hear anything. Based on the man's pace — and his lack of distraction en route — Jonah was sure this tea shop had been his destination.

After a twenty-count, Jonah turned and walked into the shop.

The inside was dark, lit only by the light from the street. It smelled like incense or strong tea. And it was very… small. Only a couple meters across.

Jonah could immediately see the entire place. And the man wasn't here. He looked around for another exit. But there was only a beaded doorway behind the counter. Jonah pulled out his gun and silencer and began threading it onto the barrel's end. He looked over his shoulder and walked behind the counter, holding the gun casually in his right hand, down by his side.

Behind the counter, he could see a storeroom through the beads. He walked through them, letting them ripple around him. The small back room was about the same size as the shop.

Still no man. Just boxes and other supplies.

And then he saw it.

The rug had a large lump, like it had recently been moved. He reached down with his left hand, while still keeping his gun trained on the spot on the floor. He lifted the rug and could see a false floor below it.

"There you are," he whispered to himself.

The trap door had a handle built into it, flush with the floor. He flipped the rug out of the way and pulled the trap door up — all the while letting his gun lead the way. The hole below the floor was pitch black. All he could see were the steps leading into it. He pushed the trap door open, wide enough to stay without needing to be propped. With one more look over his shoulder, he walked down into the dark hole in the floor.

5

THE VAULT

It took her a moment to process those words.

"Here," she said. "Like *down* here, right now?"

He nodded and ducked back through the metal door, backing out of the small room and going into the outer room.

Erin got up, almost knocking over a stack of papers in the process.

The room just outside the one Erin had been in was the buffer between the locked room and the twisty hall leading up to Sabeer's false floor in his shop. Off to the side, there was a computer at a small desk. It was a security system, Erin noticed. And it looked like it was installed back sometime around the year computers entered the public market. Erin hadn't paid much attention to it when she'd first arrived, thinking it was just piled up storage. But now, she saw the screen, where Sabeer had wiped a heavy layer of dust away. And it was on. As she looked closer, she could see the monitor was divided into quadrants. Cameras. She looked up to the closed wooden door, leading to the tunnel. One of the cameras, she saw from the screen, was just outside that door.

"Paul had me install these," he told her. "But last year, I also installed a few additions. Actually, at Paul's insistence. Tripwires," he told her.

"Tripwires?" she said.

"They tell me if someone goes somewhere in my shop they shouldn't. Such as opening one of the trap doors without using the hidden button."

Erin was watching the screen. They were all four frozen. No motion. But Sabeer's phone was still in his hand. He was staring at the monitor.

"I just got the alert," he said.

"Are you sure it's—" she said, looking at him.

"Yes," he whispered quickly, not looking at her. He continued to stare at the glass black and white monitor screen. His body was tense.

Erin looked back to the room she'd just come from, and then to the door in front of them. The outer door was wooden. She felt like a good shove may knock it down. And while the interior door was metal, she wasn't sure it would hold up against the right kind of force. This place was protected by secrecy, not force. And now, that might be in jeopardy.

"Sabeer," she whispered.

He didn't answer. He was still staring at the monitor.

Then Sabeer looked up, as if he remembered something.

"Light," he said, pointing to the other side of the room.

She looked at him.

"Now," he said, pointing.

She walked the short distance across the outer room and flipped the light. The wooden door to the hall was shut, and there was a small latch on it. She locked it, just in case. Not that it would do much. She didn't even know who she was locking out. Or if there was even anyone there. Paul had been secretive to the point of paranoia. And while, after looking through his paperwork, she understood his caution. She wasn't so sure if Sabeer wasn't a little too on edge.

As she turned back around, she could only see his face, lit up by the ancient monitor.

She walked back to the monitor, and stood beside him. She still felt this was a bit of an over-reaction. She knew his tripwires weren't old. But everything down here felt old. She figured something was probably just malfunctioning.

"Sab—" she said, and then stopped talking.

She was staring at the monitor.

Erin saw the shoulder of a man walk past the first camera.

Sabeer was completely still.

Someone else was here.

6

EXIT

ERIN LOOKED BACK BEHIND HER, TO THE YELLOW LIGHT pouring out of Paul's dusty vault. She turned back to Sabeer, still staring at the monitors.

"We've got to get out of here," she said.

He looked at her and then back to the monitor. "Paul was clear. If this" — he waved his hand behind him — "was discovered, we'd have to abort it all."

"Fine," Erin said. "Let's go. Is there a—"

"No," Sabeer interrupted, pointing to a wire that went along the floor and into the vault. "Abort. Destroy."

"You mean…"

Sabeer nodded. "It's rigged to blow. We can't come back once we leave."

Erin looked back to the room. The stacks of research. Her own stack she'd made of everything she needed to scan and save. Everything that would be vital to not only prove the conspiracy behind her mother's murder, but a half a dozen other crimes by Eli Bren. And, as well — a thought she was growing increasingly uncomfortable with — those stacks held the identity of her father. Then she looked back at the flimsy wooden door, the only thing separating them from whoever had found the passageway.

Erin immediately ran back into the vault, passing her latest stack of papers. She was opening dusty cabinets and turning over old containers. Sabeer looked over his shoulder at her.

"What are you looking for?" he whispered.

"This," she said, holding up a dark tan duffel bag. Dust fell off of it as she picked it up.

"Make it fast," he said, looking back at the monitor.

Erin ran back to the desk she'd spent the last few hours sitting at. She pushed the chair out of the way, knocking it to the ground. With two hands, she picked up the entire stack of papers she's spent the afternoon stacking and dumped it into the duffel.

"Sabeer," she said while she worked. "Please tell me there's a back door to this place."

"Yes, but…," he said.

"But what?"

"It's rigged, too."

"What do you mean?"

"As soon as it's opened," he said. "A timer starts. And then detonation."

"How long?"

"Twenty seconds."

"Twenty seconds," Erin repeated, stopping to look at him. "That's not long enough."

"It'll have to be," he said, not looking at her.

She looked back over at Paul's research and then the duffel bag. She moved to a different section of her work station, choosing, as best she could tell, the vital folders and stacks. The duffel was filling quickly. She tugged on the straps, feeling its weight already surprisingly heavy.

"Can't you disable it and do it remotely or something?" she said.

"No," he whispered. He was still watching the monitor from just outside the inner room Erin was in. "It's part of the failsafe. It's meant for exactly this kind of situation."

Erin swore. No longer bothering to keep her's to a whisper.

"Erin," Sabeer hissed from the next room. "He's at camera two. *Hurry.*"

She saw her laptop under a stack of papers. Almost forgetting it, she picked it up and tossed it into the duffel. Then she stopped, and looked around the room. Looking at the charts on the wall. The news clippings. Paul Dannon's life work. She zipped the duffel, and with a heave, she lifted it up onto the desk.

Sabeer stuck his head in. "*Now,*" he said, walking into the room.

"Alright," Erin said. "I'm ready."

"This way," he said.

She heaved the bag over her shoulder.

Sabeer walked to a rack of shelving on the other side of the room. He pulled on the shelving, leveraging his body. He let out a grunt, no longer concerned with keeping his voice down. And another pull and the shelving fell crashing down. The books and binders on it falling to the ground, a few papers floating with a new cloud of dust. They both coughed. For a moment it was hard to see. Erin pulled the neck of her shirt up, covering her mouth. Sabeer heaved the rest of the shelving out of the way, revealing another door. He stepped in front of it. But then he turned and looked back at her.

"Another lock," he said.

"You've got to be…" she said. "Did Paul give you the keys?"

"No," he said, looking back at it. "It's a combination lock."

She swore again. "How many digits?"

"Just four," he said. He was already trying combinations.

"Can we break it?" she said.

"Only if we were in the movies," he said, trying another combination and pulling it. Still locked.

"I have an idea," she said, dropping the duffel and pulling out her phone.

He turned to look at her.

"Try this," she said. "It's the code — the GPS coordinates for your shop. The ones Paul sent me."

She showed him the phone.

"It's too long," he said, shaking his head.

"Try parts of it," she said.

Erin handed him the phone and ran back to the monitor, leaving Sabeer to work on combinations. As she walked up to the monitor, she saw someone's shoulder pass in front of one of the cameras. It was the third square screen. Bottom left.

"Sabeer," she called out without taking her eyes off "are these monitors in order?"

"Yes," he called back. Then it was his turn to swear. "This isn't working," he called out.

"Keep trying, Sabeer," she said. "We've got seconds. He's very close."

Erin was watching the bottom right square on the screen. The fourth camera. The one that was pointing down directly in front of the door a meter and a half in front of her. She hadn't noticed any cameras when they came down. But then, it had been pretty dark. She wasn't sure how far spaced out they were. But the tunnel wasn't that long.

She could feel her heart beating in front of her.

"Sabeer?" she hissed.

He didn't answer.

Then the fourth square changed.

A flash.

It looked like the monitor flickered. But it was only that square. Only that camera flashed.

Then it did it again.

Erin's mouth was dry. So dry she couldn't even taste the dust anymore. Or swallow.

"Okay," Sabeer called out. "That did it. The lock's open," he yelled.

Erin repositioned, as if ready to run. But she couldn't take her eyes off the screen. Not yet. Because… The person who'd tripped the wires — who Sabeer had seen walk through the earlier cameras — was now standing in full view of the fourth camera.

The camera could see his face now, lit by the light above the wooden door. The one she was just behind.

And even in that small black-and-white square on the monitor, he was unmistakable.

She knew him.

That thin, manicured build.

His narrow face. Light slicked-back hair.

Through the monitor, she could see him standing just a few feet from her. On the other side of the wooden door. He was holding a gun down by his side.

Everything inside her was going into overdrive.

It was Jonah Lennox.

7

FBI HEADQUARTERS

HALE WALKED THE OFFICE-BEIGE HALLS HE KNEW WELL. He could have been in any building on the east coast, plain as it was. But, as it turns out, he was in the FBI headquarters in Washington D.C. And for the better part of a decade, that had been exactly where he wanted to be.

Except for today.

Or, more accurately, except for today since 10:12 — eight minutes ago, as he looked down at his vintage Casio — which was when he got a call from his boss, Mickey Eldridge.

Hale saw the call coming in and picked up, without thinking much about it. By then, he'd been back in the office for a few days. The Colombia stuff had drawn a lot of attention. But none of that heat had shifted its way back to Hale. And for an organization that seemed to be full of bureaucrats and PR-focused paper-pushers, that was saying something.

He filed his report yesterday afternoon, reading it first start-to-finish three times before sending it in. There was nothing incriminating there, he was sure of it. Paul Dannon had gone rogue, simple as that. And there was nothing Hale could have done about it. Dannon was well-vetted by the

Bureau, and he came with a long history from the CIA. And, last Hale heard, local authorities were investigating the events that happened at the top of Eli Bren's tower, which further pushed the idea that this wasn't a bad-apple situation. Some locals even reported gunshots.

Hale, of course, knew exactly what happened on the rooftop. And he knew that everyone, starting with his boss, Mick, and on up the chain, also knew exactly what happened.

But none of that made it into Hale's report.

And, as far as he could tell, there was no connection back to him. Which is why this morning's call worried him so much. Mick, after all, didn't normally call and talk about case reports.

"Need to talk to you about the Colombia report," Mick had said when Hale answered his phone this morning. Short and to the point, like always. But something was… different. There was a softness in his voice. A lack of urgency. And to Hale, that meant only one thing: Whatever was coming next would be one-way. Mick hadn't called Hale in to get information from him. He'd called him in to give him more information. And that's what had Hale on edge.

Hale walked up to Mick's office. The door was open, so he knocked twice on the metal frame. Mick looked up from his desk. If there was a standard caricature of a bureaucrat, Mickey Eldridge was it. Dark suit, white shirt, dark tie. Every day, same outfit. Take that away, and if you meet him at a bar-b-que, you'll immediately forget him. Plain face. Plain hair. And a plain personality. In short, it was exactly the kind of person who did well in the Bureau.

"Tom," Mick said, looking up from his desk. "Come in." He waved him in with his pen. "Have a seat, have a seat." His voice was casual.

Hale pulled out one of the chairs facing Mick's desk and

sank into it. Mick slid his paperwork away and folded his hands in front of him, looking at Hale.

"Listen, Tom, eh, what I—" Mick started, and then shifting gears: "Thanks for filing the report so quickly."

"Uh, sure thing, Mick," Hale said.

"Right. So…what I called you in for is… well, upstairs" — he pointed with his pen — "they're getting, uh, let's say, *antsy* about this whole thing."

"The whole thing? You mean, Colombia?"

"Yeah," Mick said. "You know, because of the pending Defense contract with Eli Bren. It was *his* building that made it into your report. And then, the part about local investigations being ongoing. All that stuff…you know how they are."

Hale really had tried to make it as vanilla as possible. If he'd left anything else out, it would have drawn suspicions. Looked like a cover-up.

"So…," Hale started, "You want me to change something in the report?"

"No, no," Mick said. "Nothing like that."

Mick seemed to be stalling. Like he didn't want to say something. Hale decided to let him keep trying on his own. He had a feeling he knew where this was going. Hale put his hands together in his lap and then moved them back to his side and then finally propped them back up on the armrests. It was a chair that seemed to be designed *not* to be used for sitting.

"Here's the thing, Tom," Mick said. "I have to suspend you."

"Suspend me?" Hale said. His voice was level. This had been his suspicion since he got Mick's call. He'd heard rumors of this kind of stuff happening. But he always wrote it off as office gossip. "What…for?" Hale said.

Mick sighed.

"It's…," Mick started. "It's political. You ask me—" he

said and stopped, looking behind Hale at the open door. Then, lowering his voice, he stared again: "You ask me, they don't want anyone anywhere near this whole Eli Bren situation. They've already picked their man. They've done their due-diligence — so they say — and they don't want anyone messing with it. Especially not someone highlighting something they missed. Like I said, political."

"So," Hale said. "What does this mean?"

"It means," Mick said, "Stay away. Trust me on this one. This is for your own good."

Hale didn't respond. What was there to respond to…

Mick looked down and slid his paperwork back in front of him: Hale's signal to leave. Hale stood up and walked to the door.

"Tom," Mick said.

Hale stopped and turned.

"Take my advice on this one and *don't* talk about this. No one."

Hale nodded.

"I'm serious. It's… it's that kind of thing."

Hale turned and walked out.

8

FATHER

THE EXIT OUT OF PAUL'S UNDERGROUND ROOM WAS A straight shot upward. As Erin climbed the ladder, she hadn't realized how far underground they were. They must be at least twenty feet down, she thought. The tunnel was dark and the ladder was rusty. She could hear Sabeer climbing below her.

"It's starting," Sabeer said.

Erin could feel the heat. She climbed faster. Her hand scraped the ceiling. "I'm at the top," she said. She'd felt above her. It was hard, dark and solid. She pushed upward, and, to her relief, the hatch opened without any fuss. Or, more accurately, it slid open. The top of the shaft was an unattached metal cover.

She climbed out and found herself next to a roadside cafe. She looked back to the hole from where she'd just come. It was disguised to look like a manhole cover.

Sabeer pushed the duffel up, and Erin grabbed the straps and used her weight to pull it out. He quickly lifted himself out, and the two of them slid the manhole cover back in place. Erin could feel the heat radiating out.

A few people were watching them. And then Erin felt the thump as a heavy vibration shook the ground. Paul must have rigged it to catch on fire before exploding.

The two of them stood up.

"Go," Sabeer said. "Don't try to contact me, not for a while. They'll be watching."

Sabeer turned to leave.

"What about you?" she said.

He turned back to her. "I'll be fine," he said. "Don't worry about me. Do what you need to do." He eyed the bag down by her feet as he said the last part.

She nodded as he turned to go. She reached down and hefted the duffel, and flung it over her shoulder. She looked around her. She recognized where she was. Before she'd found Sabeer, she spent a couple days in the city. She positioned the duffel to a more comfortable position and started walking. There was an internet cafe not far. The sun was beginning to set.

Erin looked at her watch. She pulled out her phone and dialed Ben.

"Hey," he said.

"I've got it," she said.

"All of it?"

"Enough of it. There was…," she looked around as she said it, "a complication."

"What kind of complication?"

"I'll tell you all about it soon. But there's something else. Something I… I don't know. I'm not sure I—"

"What?"

She was walking on a sidewalk in downtown Tangier. Cars were moving past her over on her right side. She stopped at an intersection, waiting for an opening in the traffic. She found a space between cars and kept walking.

"Well," she said. "Paul kept records on a lot of things."

"Uh-huh."

"And…," she was having a hard time getting it out. It was all so bizarre. Not the conspiracy — that had a mess of problems all its own. It was the side story. The part where Paul named her father. And, more specifically, the *person* he named.

"Spit it out," Ben said.

"It's Eli Bren."

"Yeah, no kidding."

"No," she said. "I mean, in Paul's notes, he says it was Eli Bren. Who is… who is my father."

Ben was silent.

"I don't understand," he said. "How could that even—"

"I don't know," Erin said. "I didn't get as much time as I wanted, to look through it all. But apparently, he and my mom were…" She didn't even want to think about that.

"Wow," Ben said. "That's…"

"Yeah," she said. "I mean, that's what Paul believed anyway. And… he was right about a lot of other stuff. He had notes and copies of a lot of classified documents. Why else would he have that in a place like this if it *wasn't* true. Right?"

"Eli Bren…," Ben repeated. "Is your dad."

He sounded skeptical. Erin didn't blame him. She would be skeptical. But she wasn't…*anything*. It's like she was in shock or something. Like she was reading a movie script about a story that was hers. But not real life. And definitely not *her* life.

"I still don't understand how that could have even happened," he said.

"The part I had the chance to read was that he and my mom were having an affair," she said. "He was ending his current relationship. She was an up-and-coming journalist.

And he was, from appearances, a respectable businessman, who was also making strides in the world."

"But…," Ben said. "I mean, how *old* was he?"

"At the time, around forty, I think. Maybe a few years older. But mom was younger. In her mid-late twenties when I was born. Paul didn't go into the details. Just the facts."

"I guess that could work…," Ben said.

"I don't know," Erin said. "It's all so—"

"Bizarre," Ben finished.

Bizarre was true. But it didn't do it justice. Though she couldn't think of any word that did. What a family she had… She had finally found the person ultimately responsible for her mother's murder. The man who instigated and funded it all — and Paul's documentation was meticulous on this point — and then, in almost the same breath, she learned that that same person was her… her *father*.

"Look," she said into the phone. "I can't think about this right now."

"Right," he said.

She stopped and looked, crossing another street.

"So you're doing it then," Ben said.

"Yeah," she said, moving the duffel bag farther up her shoulder. The sun was dipping below the tips of the buildings. Night was coming.

"Okay then," he said. "Just watch your back."

"I'll call you when it's done," she said, and she hung up.

9

GAVIN

"Gavin," she called from somewhere else in the house. Somehow, in spite of her age, her voice carried remarkably well. "Gavin, I need you."

Since everything in Ghana went down, Gavin Melton hadn't been able to get a job. Or even freelance work. No one would touch him. He graduated from MIT with a degree in data science, interned at Massachusetts General, an industry leader in cutting edge technology, and then went on to do a stint in the Peace Corps. He had a resume that made finding a job a breeze.

And yet, he'd been blackballed.

He didn't know why, or even how. But as soon as he came back from Ghana, no one would return his calls. It was only when he reached out to an old school friend, that heard someone actually say the words: "No one will touch you." It was hard to hear. But at least he knew it wasn't his imagination. There was a rumor that SERA, the nonprofit Paul Dannon was running in Ghana, was corrupt and manipulating data at the hazard of indigenous farmers. And because he was the resident data scientist on Paul's team, the industry was collectively blaming him. It didn't matter that the rumors were false. Or that there was no proof of any of it. Or that, in fact, there was proof to the *contrary*, that they were *exposing* the fraud, not creating it. All anyone seemed to care about was that he was involved in a controversy. He had his own theories about this. There was someone behind it. There had to be. These things don't spread this far and this fast. And certainly not in the harmonious chorus he'd been hearing. But, whatever the actual reason behind it, the reality was: now he couldn't get a job.

Well… that wasn't entirely true.

"Gavin, honey?" she called again.

"Yeah," Gavin mumbled, "be right there."

Millicent Beaumont was heiress to an east coast fortune. One of those never-married, old-money types. The kind who had an inheritance that seemed to have its own personality — as if it too was a member of the family.

But he needed cash. It was as simple as that. And if it meant doing IT work for a wealthy, private client — which was 90% answering questions about how to reset passwords and attach files to emails — then he'd do it.

That was two months ago.

Now, he was about to his breaking point.

This week he'd been installing a security system. It was a job that should have taken two hours. He was going on day-four, mostly because Millicent Beaumont couldn't make up her mind. It was the equivalent of a fussy homeowner giving movers a steady stream of new instructions on where to put the couch. And while the work was hardly the challenge he was looking for, it gave him moments of silence. Mostly, this week, those moments were spent installing another camera at another angle over another door, or running more ethernet cable through the attic. The attic was where Gavin was right now. But, upon hearing his name, he'd have to stop that, go down, and help Millicent Beaumont turn on her computer. Or maybe turn it off this time.

She called his name again.

"Alright," he said, "I'm coming." He dropped the spool of ethernet and looked at the hole in the attic floor that led back into the house. It was a ten-foot drop. He had a ladder set up. But he thought seriously about just falling through the hole and seeing where that got him. It'd be an accident, of course. And if he survived, maybe there would be some clause in that ridiculously long and obtuse contract she made him sign that would set him up for life. A life far, far away. "I'm coming," he said, his voice barely above a sigh, as he put his hands on the two-by-fours above the hole and slipped back down onto the ladder. The attic wasn't insulated, and so it was cold. As he slipped down into the regular area, he could feel the warmth from Millicent Beaumont's heater. The hot, stuffy always-running heater.

Just like hell.

THE VESPER PROTOCOL

ERIN PULLED HER LAPTOP OUT OF THE DUFFEL BAG SHE was carrying, and slid the bulky bag under the table. She was sitting, with her back in a corner, at a 24-hour coffee shop. Most of the people around her were sitting with laptops, headphones, and coffee. She was sitting with a view of the door. Other than offering free internet, it was a good place to regroup. It was quiet. And everyone here seemed pretty low keyed, consumed with their own private world in their laptops. Anyone who'd come for her wouldn't be hard to spot.

She logged into a VPN — a digital tunnel, designed to hide web traffic from any would-be spies. *The Washington Post* required her to use one of these for all of her communications and uploads. Back then, it seemed like overkill. But now, with everything that had been going on, she'd hoped it was enough. It connected, giving her a little green light, telling her that all was clear.

She pulled up her email. One immediately caught her eye.

From: The Office of Senator Cleason

It was the aide she'd been corresponding with. Before she came to Tangier, while still in Bogotá, she — along with the help and resources of her editor at the *Post*, Conall McGillis — had done some digging. Apparently, Eli Bren was heavily tied to Senator Avery Cleason. And it was Cleason who was pushing the Defense contract through in Washington. A week ago, after the events that happened at the top of Bren's tower, she immediately started a correspondence with Senator Cleason's office. As a *Washington Post* reporter — even a stringer — she had enough credibility to get a few responses. But it had been slow.

She opened the email and read its single line of text:

Thank you for your interest in this matter, but Senator Cleason is not able to comment at this time.

Translation: *We already know everything we want to know, and we're not looking for information that doesn't conform to what we're already doing.* Typical.

She'd mostly expected this answer. Her goal wasn't to get immediate cooperation from them, though that would have been nice. Her goal was to get the conversation started and set a baseline. These sorts of things were always a part of a process. And, to the credit of their response, so far Erin hadn't given them any hard and fast *proof.* She, of course, had seen first hand what Bren was capable of. She'd been there when Val shot and killed Paul — Bren condoning the whole thing. But she couldn't report on that. Not yet. Not until she had something more substantial, something money and lawyers couldn't overcome.

She looked up, over her laptop screen, to check for any watcher. Anyone who wasn't sufficiently absorbed in their own screen. Satisfied, she reached under her seat and pulled out the duffel bag. She dropped it into the chair next to her and unzipped it. She began looking through the contents, pushing dusty papers aside, without taking out anything she didn't have to. She found a few of the folders she was looking for. She slipped them out and set a small stack on top of the duffel bag. One at a time, she opened them, found the critical pages she needed and took pictures with her phone. She transferred them to her computer using the cafe's wifi, knowing it wasn't a secure transfer, but taking the chance since she didn't have a cord to transfer safely.

Back on her laptop, she clicked reply to the email from Senator Cleason's aide and attached the images of the documents she just took.

Please see attached.

These are a few documents that back-up the story I'm writing — the one we previously spoke about. There are quite a few more, spread out among several safe boxes. But I trust these will sufficiently explain the nature of this unfolding story.

I urge Senator Cleason to discuss this matter with me, so that we may find a way to run this article in a way that is not damning to Senator Cleason or his office. His cooperation would be greatly appreciated.

She signed her name and held her breath. She waited, her finger hovering over the button that would send the email.

These were strong words. It was a polite but clear way of saying: we've got evidence of your misdeeds, the evidence is safe from your tampering, and if you don't cooperate, we'll use it and you'll regret it. Not much different than most ransom notes, when she thought of it. Except, in this case, Erin hadn't stolen anything.

Still, there was a fine line. And she knew it. If a judge later ruled that she had something to gain in this whole thing, then this would probably be seen as a clear-cut attempt to extort a sitting United States senator.

Before she clicked send, she opened a new window and wrote a different email to her editor, McGillis:

Conall, see attached. Sending this to Cleason now. More where this is coming from. No time to send it all to you right now. But I will. I've found what we were looking for.

Talk soon,

-E

She went back to the first email — the one to the Cleason's aide — and read it again. She glanced up and took another look around the coffee shop. She thought she saw a man look away when she looked at him. But then, he could have thought the same thing about her. She was having a hard time distinguishing between paranoia and prudence. She let out a slow breath. "Focus, Erin," she told herself.

She hovered her mouse over the Cleason email and clicked send. Her computer made a whooshing sound effect. And she watched the ticker in the corner of her email — the feature that gave her five seconds to click undo and stop the email from sending. She watched the counter go down to zero, and then, it was gone. She closed the lid to her laptop and slid it and the folders back into the duffel bag.

She knew, what came next, that would be the really hard part.

11

EL DORADO INTERNATIONAL AIRPORT

Val sat in an airport chair, dressed in a dark pinstripe skirt and white blouse, legs crossed, as the terminal around her began to fill up. She looked down at her watch. Twenty minutes until the gate attendant opened up boarding. People, mostly men, were filing in, filling up the seats around her. From their dress — and some of them who were still wearing their lanyards — it looked like a large conference had just ended. That wasn't unusual for Bogotá.

Across from her, a man sat down. Conference attendee. Still young. Probably in his late twenties. She made eye contact, more from boredom than anything else.

He returned the look, letting his eyes linger. Something she was accustomed to. He was in good shape. Like he prioritized the gym, even on vacation — but not like he ever had real-world exercise. She figured, if pushed, he'd crumble. Probably fast.

She turned away and looked out of the large floor-to-ceiling windows and watched her plane, as the gangway was being fitted to its open door. She could still feel the man looking at her, trying to make eye contact with her again.

She looked back at him, before leaning down, slowly. She zipped her bag on the floor in front of her, preparing for the gate attendant's call in a few minutes. She pulled a pen out as she sat back up.

The boy across from her had sat forward too, resting his arms on his knees. He smiled. More cocky than kind.

"Marco," he said.

She gave him a sympathetic smile, and looked away. There really was something about these, these *gallos*, that she enjoyed. Too cocky for their own good. They rarely made it far. And they never saw the part that was coming next.

She didn't bother telling him her name. That was the bait. Not that she had any plans for him — for "Marco." But there were certain luxuries a woman with her tastes had a hard time passing up.

"You going to D.C.?" Marco said.

She looked back at him.

"Are you?" she said slowly.

"Yeah," he said. He handed her his card. She was genuinely impressed by how fast he produced it. Like he was a professional card-giver. Probably was.

She took it with one hand and looked at it. "Mmm," she said, looking back up at him. "A lawyer?" She said it like she was impressed, letting her Spanish accent come out. She could tell he enjoyed that. She was exotic. And he was already too far in to turn back.

He turned casually and looked out the window. She kept looking at him. The tiniest of smiles curled at the corner of his mouth. One he was no doubt doing his best to hide. "Junior partner," he said. "Right now, anyway."

"That's impressive," she said, leaning forward again.

He looked at her again. For which, he didn't have much choice. Val was in charge. She'd been in charge since he sat down.

She reached her hand out, offering him the card back.

"Keep it," he said. "Never know."

She put it inside the little pocket on her shirt. Her white blouse was slightly transparent, and she figured he could see its outline. He was looking at it, anyway.

"So—" he said, doing his best to bring his eyes back up to hers. "So, you…live in D.C., or just visiting?"

"Visiting," she said.

She knew he knew that before she answered. He was setting her up. Or trying to. She knew the game. She'd played it a thousand times. Only difference was, she was *good* at it.

"Pleasure?" he said.

"Business," she said. "But pleasure when I can get it."

He cleared his throat again. "I've been there for a while now. I live near Foggy Bottom. Know it? Doesn't matter. We should connect — while you're there," he added.

"Should we?" she said, raising an eyebrow.

She was the cat. Long and experienced. If only he knew he was the mouse. She fiddled with the pen in her hand.

"Yeah," he said. "I can show you around. Show you…the city."

"You can do that?" she said.

He reached down and grabbed the handles on his leather bag and moved across to sit in the seat next to her. He leaned on the armrest between them. She turned only her head to watch him. She sat back. He smelled like sweet cologne.

"Yeah," he said, "We can do all kinds of things."

"That's kind of you," she said, still playing with the pen.

"What eh, what did you say your name was?" he said.

Her phone buzzed in her bag below. She leaned down and picked it up, knowing he'd be following each of her curves as she moved.

She smiled at him as she sat back up. "I didn't," she said, as she answered her phone.

He smiled back and looked away, letting her take the call. He was winning.

"Yes," she said into her phone. It was Eli on the other end.

Val leaned forward to talk.

"This secure?" Eli asked.

"No."

"There's been a…complication," he said.

"How?" she said, still fingering the ink pen.

"The package is out."

"And the carrier?" she said.

"Her, too," Eli said.

Val looked down at her watch. More out of habit than to actually learn something from it. She didn't expect a call from her man yet. But often, in a job like this, there were a few layers to work through. So that wasn't a red flag.

"How do you know?" she asked Eli.

"Because I'm looking at an email she sent fourteen minutes ago. Forwarded from the senator directly. With very incriminating pictures attached. And he's not happy," Eli added.

She was about to respond to Eli, when she stopped. She felt Marco's hand touch her. Her skin, on her shoulder, just where her blouse ended. She turned sharply, the phone still at her ear, and looked at him. He had his arm resting on the back of their chairs, and his fingers dangling down. Pleasure — and her games — would have to wait.

She gave him a look, one she was sure he didn't understand. Control was about imbalance. He didn't remove his hand. So she put her other hand, the one still holding the pen, on his leg next to her. Tapping him and then taking her hand back. But not her gaze. She left that on him as she continued to talk to Eli.

"What do you want me to do?" she said, still holding the phone.

Marco smiled at her.

In her ear, Eli was telling her they'd need to change plans. The specifics, of course, he couldn't go into over an un-secure line.

Marco, meanwhile, looked over his shoulder, to the list of departure times. Calculating, no doubt, how long they had before the plane left.

She put her hand, still holding the pen, on his thigh and left it there this time.

He grinned wider.

She slipped her hand between his legs.

His smile faltered a little bit as he adjusted slightly in his seat. She could tell she was already pushing him further than he was used to being pushed. This was his first point he realized he might not be in control.

And then, she did what he didn't expect. She pushed the pen back, down farther between his legs. It was a heavy, metal pen. The kind that would make a clank if it fell to the floor. His face shifted. He wasn't smiling anymore. He didn't know what to do. She pushed more, feeling resistance. He was confused. And a little worried. This had gone bad, fast. And he didn't know how to stop it.

"Wha—" he started, keeping his voice low.

She mouthed "shhh" to him.

He sat frozen, pushed as far back in the seat next to her, as he could.

In her ear, Eli asked her when she would be in D.C.

She looked past Marco, relieving him of no pressure, and looked at the digital read-out of flight times. "Plane boards in about ten minutes," she said. "Leaving Bogotá can be tricky," she said, now looking back at Marco. "But," she released the pressure, but only slightly, "I don't think I'll have any more delays."

Marco tightly shook his head no. She smiled. She could still see multiple levels of discomfort on his face. Eli hung up the phone. And she pulled it down. She let go of the pen, letting it fall between his legs.

"That's my card," she said. "And you can keep it."

Marco was breathing in tight control bursts.

She looked back forward. He was still, not moving.

"You can go now," she said.

He immediately picked up his bag and left.

She didn't watch him go, though a tiny smile did appear on her lips. She sat, like she was before Marco joined her, and waited for the next few minutes to pass before it was time to board.

12

BEN

BEN TOOK THE STEPS OUT OF THE METRO TWO AT A time. He crossed a busy Pennsylvania Avenue, feeling the cold chill hit him. He walked down D Street and then turned left onto 8th, heading to his third library this week. The last few days had felt more like he was back in school, doing a research project or something. Even more so, because he couldn't use Google, or the internet, to help him. Since Ben had come back from Bogotá, he'd been staying at Erin's place in D.C. while she was in Morocco. Upon checking his email, he found a message waiting for him.

From Paul.

He almost didn't click it. It couldn't have been… Not really… Paul was—

He looked at the date and did a quick calculation in his head. It was sent right around the same time he'd gotten the text from Paul. Just before Paul…

He sat there for a moment looking at it. But ultimately, it was the subject line that caused his curiosity to win out. It was a single word: *Vesper.*

He clicked it. Inside were two more words, "click here," underlined in blue as a hyperlink. If this email had been advertising Viagra or 'investment opportunities,' it would be a dead ringer for spam. But knowing Paul, it was all set up long ago. Paul was always functional. Never caring much for appearances.

He clicked it.

It immediately started a download, which only took a second or two. Ben clicked the downloaded file. At first, nothing happened. Ben thought something had gone wrong. He went back to the email to try again, but it was gone. The message appeared to be deleted. Was he seeing things? He checked the deleted folder in his email. Nothing.

And then, Erin's printer behind him started making noise. It was printing something.

Ben turned back to the computer. But the file that he'd downloaded a moment ago was gone. "What in the…?" He'd heard of things like this. But he didn't believe they really existed. When he clicked on the program, it must have triggered the printing and then deleted itself. He knew crazy stuff like that was technically possible. But it was surreal seeing it happen in front of him.

He turned back at the printer and picked up the page which had finished printing now.

At the top was a message from Paul.

Ben — Your eyes only.

All traces of you getting this message will be erased.

Memorize my instructions below. Then burn the paper.

From here on out — stay offline. No exceptions.

Paul

The rest of the page was a no-nonsense list of bullet

points. Typical Paul. Straight to the point. No mention of, 'if I'm dead.' And certainly nothing sentimental. Ben smiled to himself as he thought about that. Paul was one of the last of the tough guys.

Everything Ben had been doing for the last few days had been from Paul's playlist. He'd spent a small fortune in library copy-machine fees, looking up what felt like an endlessly stupid assignment on the United States government and its contractors. But it wasn't generic overview stuff, it was all hyper-specific. Paul had left him a roadmap consisting of several starting points, and then instructions to find revenue sources, campaign funders, and contractors. His guidelines were specific: don't stop searching until the funder or backer or contractor "makes obvious sense." Ben didn't think much about that statement until he started actually doing the work. He didn't know how convoluted and shady politics could be. Sure, he had a healthy level of cynicism. Who didn't? But what he found was taking him deeper and faster than he expected. What amazed him most was how much of this stuff was written down and available for the public to find — if you knew where to look.

After only a few hours into Paul's instructions, he understood the original text Paul sent him, just before he died. "Start Vesper."

This was Vesper. Paul had planned all of it ahead of time. *Years* ahead of time.

Paul had also, proactively, put together a team. Or, earmarked a team for *Ben* to put together. Which was his next call.

He was on one of his four regular routes to the library (Paul had told him to have at least three or more routes to anything he did on a regular basis). He pulled out a go phone that he'd prepaid and dialed Gavin's number. It took an irritatingly long time to find that bit of intel without the internet. Even though the two of them had worked and lived side by side for months in Ghana in the middle of nowhere, he never had the need to actually call the guy.

The phone rang for almost a minute.

"Hello," came the answer on the end.

"Gavin, my brother, how's it going?"

"Ben? Wow, I, uh. I didn't expect to hear from you."

"A lot's happened recently," Ben said.

Gavin was quiet.

"You heard about Paul?"

"Yeah," Gavin said, quietly.

"Yeah," Ben said back.

"Crazy freak accident," Gavin said. "And Paul…of all people." Gavin was referring to the official version of Paul's death: An American tourist involved in a solo hiking accident in the remote mountains outside of Bogotá. First, American tourists don't go 'hiking' in those mountains. And second, Paul Dannon…a hiking accident? To the few that knew the truth, if the whole thing hadn't been so painful it would have been laughable.

Ben would fill him in soon. But not over the phone.

"You busy?" Ben said.

"Busy?" he said with a laugh. "No."

Ben could hear someone in the background. It sounded like she was talking to him.

"You sure? I can call ba—"

"No," Gavin said sharply. "Definitely not busy. What's up?"

Ben walked up to a busy intersection and pushed the call button on the cross-walk post. He put his free hand back in his jacket. It wasn't snowing yet. But the wind was biting. An older man stood next to him, wearing a long cashmere overcoat. He focused on his phone. Ben tilted away anyway and continued talking to Gavin.

"I've got a job I need help with," Ben said.

"I'm in," Gavin said. "Where?"

"D.C.," Ben said. "But you don't even know what—"

"I can be there in a few hours," Gavin said.

Ben smiled.

"You should know," he said. "The pay's not very good."

"Fine," Gavin said.

And that was true. There was money. Paul left all of his worldly possessions to fund what Erin and Ben — and the rest, if Ben could get them — would be doing. Fortunately, or maybe by design, most of Paul's assets had been liquid at the time of his death. Another strange part of this whole thing was that when Paul died, he'd apparently triggered a clause in a contract he had with his bank. That transferred control of his account to Ben.

"And it might be dangerous."

"Okay."

"And—"

"No," Gavin said.

"What?" Ben said.

"Sorry, not you. I've been…she wants me to take the dog to the vet now. While I'm 'On my way,' she says."

"What are you talk—" Ben started, confused.

"Nothing," Gavin said. "It's a long story. When I got back from Ghana, I was blackballed. Nobody would talk to me. Much less hire me. Except her. And I think it's going to kill me."

"Good," Ben said. "This should help with that."

"What do you mean?"

"It's about Paul," Ben said. "I'll fill you in on the rest when you get here." Ben gave Gavin Erin's address. Gavin told him he'd be there in a few hours. Before Ben hung up, he thought he could hear Gavin yelling something rude to the woman he was with. Ben smiled again. He was almost to the library now. He pulled a slip of paper out of his pocket with an address scribbled on it. He had a few quick things to look up, and then, per Paul's instructions, he'd pay Thomas Hale a visit, at his house. He was hoping that wouldn't be awkward.

13

IN PERSON

"What time did you get back?" Ben said.

He was sitting across from Erin, next to a large glass window, looking out at a residential part of D.C. The restaurant was converted from an old victorian style house. It now served only breakfast food. The sun coming through was having a greenhouse effect on them. A nice change to the crisp December wind outside.

"Late," she said. "I mean" — she yawned — "Early. This morning."

Because of the layout of the house-turned-restaurant, they had the area to themselves. Through a few more yawns Erin filled Ben in on what happened — leaving out, for now, Paul's notes about Eli Bren being her father. It was too early in the morning to get into that. Or she was too jet-lagged. Or both.

"So, you really think it was Jonah there?" Ben said.

"I *saw* him," she said. "On the camera. He was there."

"I mean," Ben started, "I believe you, I do. But…it just doesn't make sense."

"What do you mean?" Erin said.

"Well," Ben started. It sounded like he was tiptoeing around the issue. "I know he's…a wild card."

"That's mild," Erin said.

"But," Ben continued, "why would he do that? Now?"

"How about, he's got this weird relationship-slash-vendetta with…," she almost couldn't bring herself to say his name. Since she'd learned who he really was — who he was to her — even the sound of it was strange. "With Bren," she finished. "And, simply, for a while Jonah and our goals aligned. But then, when they didn't, he switched back. If he was ever on our side to begin with."

"But he didn't rat us out, when he could have," Ben said. "And he helped us collect data. From what Paul's got me tracking down, that data looks like it's going to be critical."

Erin rubbed her temples. It wasn't Ben. It was the sleep-deprived headache that had been slowly getting worse. She looked up at him.

"He shot Rafael," Erin said.

"But…he lived," Ben said. "I talked to the doctor. He said it was remarkable, that there was no real damage, other than some local nerve trauma. Look—" he said. "I hear what you're saying. All I'm saying is that it doesn't add up. I feel like we're missing something."

"Yeah," she said, looking out the window. She hadn't wanted to face that head-on. That Jonah was more complex than a traitor. She needed some part of this whole tangled mess to just stay… *simple*. She wasn't ready to agree with Ben. But he was right.

Erin didn't know how Jonah fit into this yet. Maybe Colombia was a fluke. Maybe, in some weird way, there was more to him. *Maybe* was as far as she could let that thought go for now.

The fact was, she didn't trust him. And she'd *seen* him on that camera in Morocco. He was there. Trying to get in. If he was on their side, why would he do that? No, she thought, there was something else at play here. And it didn't smell right.

"So…," Ben said. "Do you want to talk about it?"

She looked back at him.

"What?" she said, coming back to the conversation.

"Bren?" he said. "The whole he's-your-dad thing."

"Oh," she said with a sigh. "I…I don't know. It just doesn't feel real, ya know? I mean, I understand *how* it could have happened," she said. "But it was before me. And, as far as I'm concerned, just biological. Nothing more."

She looked back down. But she could still feel him watching her. Waiting for her. She looked back out the window as the waiter walked up with their food. Ben thanked the woman, and Erin started eating.

Ben wasn't talking and she was thankful for the quiet. He was good about that. He noticed things. And he knew when to drop other issues. She was thankful…for him. And then, unrequested, her thought jumped back a few weeks ago, to that lift she and Ben took, up to Montserrate, the monastery that looked out above Bogotá. How Ben had been talking about settling down.

She pulled out her phone and started thumbing through her emails while she ate. She smiled at the memory. How he'd fumbled, talking about it, trying to bring it up, but not really sure how. His awkwardness was probably half her fault, she thought. Until that point, her thoughts had been so far elsewhere. She hadn't really thought of him like *that*. Not that he wasn't cute. And since he'd stopped dying his hair pink, she smiled again, that was an improvement. She continued to thumb through her email on her phone, on the table next to her plate. But since he'd mentioned it that day, it hadn't really left her mind. She found herself coming back to it and—

Erin dropped her fork in her eggs.

"Ben," she said, not taking her eyes off her screen.

"Huh?" he said.

"He wants to meet," she said.

"Who? Sen—" Ben caught himself and lowered his voice. "Senator Cleason?"

"Yeah," she said looking up. "And it's not one of his aides. It's him personally writing to me.

"Let me see," Ben said, grabbing the phone.

Ben read the message a few times.

"He just sent this," Ben said. "A few minutes ago."

"Yeah," she said. "So?"

"When did you send that stuff to him? Yesterday, midday D.C. time?"

"Yeah, I think," she said, subtracting the five hours, to account for Morocco's timezone difference. And in fact, for Erin who lost those five hours on the flight back, it had really only been one long night ago — according to the clock anyway.

"What's the problem?" she said.

"Put yourself in his shoes," Ben said. "You get information like that and what's the first thing you do?"

"I don't know," she said, "vet it, I suppose."

"Right. You have your people run through it. And you'd probably need to run through a few classified sources — considering the subject matter."

"Okay…"

"There's a lot of red tape in all of that."

"Where are you going with this?"

"I'm saying, I don't trust it."

"I'm tired, Ben."

He took the liberty of thumbing through the rest of her email since yesterday.

"Look," he said. "You sent that and then you hear nothing. No emails from aides, nothing. And then the next email is from him *directly*, and it's the 'utmost importance'," he said, quoting Cleason's words, "that you meet 'immediately and in person.'"

"This is what we wanted to happen, right?" Erin said.

"I know, yes," Ben said. "But it feels like it's… too fast."

Sometime after she got back, last night or this morning — she was having a hard time keeping it straight — Ben had filled her in on his end. On the cryptic, auto-delivered email from Paul. And how he'd given him instructions about the research. And about not going online, because, if someone wasn't already, they'd soon be tracking him. Erin had had her own bouts with paranoia. She wasn't cynical about it. It was real. But…maybe…maybe she was still just a little too tired. And maybe Ben was a little *too* paranoid.

"Sometimes," she said. "Things just work out in our favor. That's not bad, is it?" She smiled as she said that.

He looked at her. But he didn't smile. He looked like he was thinking.

She reaches across the table and slides her phone back. "He wants to meet today," she said. "So I'm going to do it."

Ben still didn't respond.

"I'll make sure it's in a public place," she said. "With cameras," she smiled again.

She could tell he was trying to come at this from another angle. A different alternative. One that felt better. Safer.

He nodded, finally. "Okay."

"But in the meantime," she said, through another yawn she couldn't hold back. "I've got to get a few more hours of sleep." They left the restaurant. The cold was alarming, but refreshing. He walked her back to her house. She walked to the front door and opened it. But he didn't follow her in, saying he had more work to do.

"But, it's Sunday," she said. "Aren't the libraries closed today?"

"No library for today," he said. "Something else."

She was too tired to be curious about that. He pulled the door closed. And she could hear him lock it from the outside as she walked upstairs to immediately fall back into her bed.

14

NO

"Hale," Ben said, through cupped hands as he spoke into the crack of his closed front door. He leaned back and pounded on the door. "I know you're in there, Tom." This was now the third time he'd tried Hale at his house. Ben had done enough homework to know Hale was here. He drove a non-government Ford Explorer, white. And he knew the plates. He also knew, through a bit of low level sleuthing, that it hadn't moved in three days, at least.

"Open up," Ben yelled into the crack again.

Ben heard the lock turn. Hale opened it, leaving the chain in place, the door stopping at five inches. Hale looked through before shutting it again, unchaining it and reopening it. Hale left the door open and, without a word, walked back inside, letting Ben follow if he wanted to. Ben walked in. Hale sat on a couch and Ben leaned up against his kitchen table, not taking a seat.

His apartment was small, but it was upscale and open-format, with high ceilings, so that it didn't feel cramped. But you could still see all the living area, more-or-less, in one view. He saw carpeted stairs off to the side. It was small, but its location (and oversized crown molding) made up for that. Or, Ben figured, that was the idea.

"How long has it been since you've been outside?"

Hale looked over his shoulder, past Ben, to the window, as if checking that the outside was in fact still there.

"Today's Saturday," Hale said, in an attempt to figure out the answer.

"It's Sunday," Ben said.

That seemed to come as a genuine surprise to Hale.

"Oh," he grunted, and apparently losing track of the answer to Ben's question.

Ben looked around and saw a few empty bottles on the bar that separated the kitchen from the living area — where Hale was presently sitting.

"They uh," Ben started. "They didn't take Colombia so well then?"

Hale let out a little laugh. "No," he said, quietly, "they didn't take Colombia so well."

"What happened?"

"Nothing really, just...," he waved hands to illustrate, though it was a little more animated than the story warranted. "Just suspended me. No reason. Just government stuff...papers."

He wasn't exactly talking straight. Ben figured a sturdy amount of alcohol was still floating around in his bloodstream. He pulled up a chair from the table and sat across from him. Hale was still lounging back. Ben leaned forward. Hale returned his gaze. Confident, but not quite competent.

"Paul sent me a message—" Ben started.

"Oh forget it," Hale said, waving him off.

"You don't even know what I'm going to say," Ben said.

"The answer is no," Hale said, getting up and walking. He stopped at the window. Ben could tell the light was hurting his eyes, and his head.

"Just listen," Ben said.

Hale did more handwaving. And the back-and-forth happened a few more times. But Hale gave in — or gave up — and started to listen. Ben told him what he'd been up to. What Erin had been doing. Told him it was all, strictly speaking, hush-hush, while secretly counting on Hale's inebriated state to keep the better part of the secret. Hale was quiet. Listening, maybe. And a few times, Ben thought he was actually catching on. Buying in. Mostly, though, Hale just listened. Or, was silently pretending to listen.

"So…what do you say?" Ben said, after he'd finished.

"No," Hale said, shutting the door, leaving Ben alone on the front porch.

Ben didn't think he'd get an immediate buy-in. "Okay," he called through the closed door. "We'll be in touch then." He sighed, turned around, and zipped up his jacket.

15

___

PRETTY NICE

___

ERIN SLEPT LATE. WELL, LATER THEN SHE'D MEANT TO. It was only four in the afternoon when she woke up. After she and Ben had breakfast, she'd *meant* to get only a few hours of sleep and then wake up and do some more prep before meeting with Senator Cleason at five.

But now, once she took a shower, it was already four-thirty. And even though it was a Sunday — which she thought was weird for a meeting, but, she reasoned, people in his position and issues like this tend to prompt weird hours.

Still, she was cutting it close.

She'd pulled out a dark skirt and a light blouse. Something easy. Though, she realized after committing that this probably wasn't the most weather-appropriate choice.

She heard a horn outside. She picked up her phone and looked at it. Her car was outside and waiting. She ran downstairs and grabbed a dressy-enough jacket from whatever was hanging in the foyer. Something that would cover up her lack of ironing and maybe keep her from freezing. She pulled the door open and almost slammed directly into Gavin Melton.

Which was weird, because the last time she'd seen him was in SERA's dusty make-shift camp, miles north of Accra, Ghana.

"Oh," she said.

He seemed to be just as startled. He was standing with his hand up in the air, apparently about to knock.

"Gavin?" she said.

"Hey…Erin," he said.

He put his hand down, apparently realizing he was still holding it, now for no reason at all.

"So…?" she said.

"Ben, uh. He didn't tell you I was coming, did he?"

She smiled. "Must have slipped his mind," she said.

She'd never been *that* close to Gavin. But it wasn't a trust thing. He was one of Paul's guys. So she knew he was good. And if Ben trusted him too, all the better. No, it was more a social thing. The two of them had never actually been alone together, and had, as far as Erin could find, nothing to talk about it.

The two of them stood for a moment. Gavin seemed to notice for the first time that she was dressed up. That she wasn't wearing khaki shorts and an old t-shirt, which, up to this point had been the only way he'd ever seen her.

"Oh, wow," he said. "You look… pretty, um — I mean, nice," he said. "No, pretty nice. How are you—" He took a deep breath to stop himself from talking

She smiled.

"Thanks, Gavin."

He recovered.

And then, thanks to the car horn at the street, so did she, remembering she was late. "Gavin," she said. "Ben's not here right now. And I've got to be somewhere, of which I am already late. Do you have somewhere to…," she started. "You know what, never mind." She handed him her keys. "Ben should be back soon."

He took the keys. And she walked past him, down the few steps leading up to her porch and opened the car's back door. She got in and tossed her jacket onto the seat next to her. She looked back at Gavin, who was still standing on the front porch in the same spot, with her front door open behind him.

"Gavin?" she called, before shutting car the door.

"Yeah?" he called back.

"Go in and shut the door, would you?"

"Oh yeah, right, okay," he said.

She smiled again as she shut the car door, and the driver pulled away.

16

LATE

Erin's car pulled up to the Dirkson Senate Office Building, a large square thing, just a few blocks from the iconic Supreme Court and Capital buildings. As far as famous government buildings went, this one was the forgotten stepbrother.

She looked down at her watch. 5:02 p.m. She swore under her breath. "This is good," she said to the driver, who stopped without parking. Erin opened the door, and felt the cold air hit her. She got out, grabbing her jacket and pulling it on as she walked. She moved as quickly as she could without breaking into a run — something that would have been awkward at best, given her choice of shoes.

She walked up to the large square building. There was a guard standing outside. She smiled at him as she walked up to the door. He nodded and walked over to the door, opening it for her. It was a little bit out of his way. She wondered if he did that for everyone. Or if the disheveled way she felt on the inside was how she looked on the outside, too. There were splashes of shiny brass in the building's architecture. She tried to discreetly find her reflection on one of them. No luck. She kept moving.

She walked to the metal detector and dropped her wallet and jacket on the conveyor belt. She walked through the detection frame and stood while a guard passed a wand over her front and back. He gave her the sign to pick up her things along with the spiel about no cameras or pictures. Though, she couldn't help noticing with a touch of irony, that there were a lot of cameras in this building.

The inside of the building didn't have much of a lobby. It was filled, floor to ceiling with marble, and all the doors were of the same shiny brass. It was a strange picture of wealth: one entirely walled off from the public, for private use, but, ironically, all publicly funded.

She moved forward, heading down a hall, following a sign to the elevators. Other than the fact that everything was covered in marble, the place seemed a bit underwhelming. She looked down at her watch. 5:09 p.m. She swore again, this time hearing her selection echo back to her. She looked around to see if anyone heard that. Still empty. At the elevator, she pushed the button. It lit up, but the doors didn't open. She saw a sign for stairs and walked to it. She pushed it open and ran, as best she could in her shoes, up a floor.

The second floor looked identical to the one below it. Senator Cleason's office was the first door she came to. She stopped, closed her eyes and took a breath, and then walked in.

Inside was a small reception area. It had a window and a few chairs and a man with his own desk. He looked up at her but didn't say anything.

"My name is Erin Reed," she said. "With the Wash—"

"Please wait," he said, looking at his computer and typing something into it.

"You had an appointment?"

"Yes," she said. "For five."

He looked down at his watch and back at her. As if repri-manding her.

Before she could respond, a woman came in, from around the corner. As Erin looked, she saw that this was part of a bigger office.

She looked directly at Erin. "Senator Cleason is running late, please come in." She motioned for Erin to follow her. The rest of the room, the part behind the first gatekeeper, was only a slight bit larger than the front area. The woman offered her a seat and a drink. "Thanks," Erin said sitting. The woman disappeared into another office, bringing back a coffee, black, in a small Styrofoam cup. Erin took it, thankful that she actually *liked* coffee black.

The woman disappeared again, back into her room, an off-shoot of the room Erin was now sitting in. Erin wondered how much there was to this place. Opposite of where she was sitting there was a heavy wooden door, closed. She assumed it belonged to Cleason.

She looked at her watch again. Well, she thought, at least he was late, too. She pulled out her phone to check her emails. Nothing urgent. She started a new message to McGillis, her editor. She told him she was back in D.C., tapping out a few more updates. She finished, letting him know she was in Senator Cleason's office now, waiting to meet with him. She made a mental note to call him when she got out.

Erin looked out the window, the sun was getting lower now.

The last few days had been a whirlwind. And until today, she hadn't gotten much sleep — really, she'd been in this state since before Paul had died. She'd just been going without slowing down. And until today, it had been taking its toll. She didn't realize how run down she was until she spent most of today sleeping. She was finally starting to feel like herself again.

And, added to that, she was beginning to feel optimistic. Sure, there were more questions than answers. And the Jonah Lennox part of the equation still didn't make sense. Though, the more she thought about it, the more she knew there was something else there. She knew he was involved in a deeper way. She still didn't understand what his play was in Colombia, but she didn't trust it. Ben, for his part, didn't seem convinced that Lennox wasn't still on their side. She wondered about this. Was she missing something?

She sipped her coffee, but it wasn't hot anymore. She looked down at her white cup. She'd almost finished it. She drank the last sip and walked across the small room to toss it in a small trash can in the corner. She looked at her watch again. It was almost 5:40 now. The sun was almost gone now.

At one point, earlier, the assistant — the one who brought her coffee before — came out and wordlessly shut the blinds before walking back in. Something about the woman reminded Erin of a robot. Mechanical.

The assistant walked back in.

"Senator Cleason," she said. "He is, eh, not available." She didn't meet her eyes when she said that last part. The calculating woman from a few minutes ago now seemed shifty.

"Did he say why?" Erin said.

"I'm afraid he's not available right now," she said, this time sounding a little more rehearsed.

"Well…can I wait for him?" Erin said.

"I'm afraid not," the woman said. "Someone will reach out to you to reschedule when he has time." She was back to business now.

"Excuse me," Erin said. "Have you actually talked to the Senator? About this?"

"The Senator," she repeated, a touch firmer, "is not available right now." Something seemed off in her tone. Erin was picking up an undercurrent of discomfort. Which was strange. Erin figured she did a lot of gatekeeping for the Senator, with press and lobbyists and other senators. Why the awkwardness, she wondered.

"Listen," Erin started, but the woman cut her off.

"You may leave this way," she said, motioning to another door. Erin hadn't noticed this other door before now. It was painted the same color as the walls. And it had the same square decorative molding on it that the rest of the walls did. It blended in almost perfectly. Erin could see the hinges now. But it didn't have a door nob. It was an exit-only door. The woman pushed it open, but didn't walk out. She held it for Erin to leave.

Erin walked out, and the door closed quickly behind her, as if they thought she might make a mad dash to get back in. She looked at her watch again. 5:45 p.m. She stood for a minute in the marble hall and looked around. It was empty. She walked back to the elevator, opting again for the stairs. She walked out of the front, the same way she'd come in, making eye contact with the security guard on her way out. As soon as she was outside, she pulled out her phone and called McGillis.

17

COLOMBIA

Gavin was sitting on Erin's couch. Which, in a few hours, would turn into Ben's bed. Gavin listened without interrupting as Ben recounted the entire story of Colombia, including Paul's death and why Erin had been in Morocco.

"And this guy, Eli Bren, who owns the shipping company—"

"And a bunch of other stuff," Ben added.

"Right. He's…Erin's dad, but…she didn't know that until just now?"

"Uh-huh," Ben said.

"And Paul *did* know it," Gavin continued. "But didn't tell her, because he was working on a larger case against this guy."

"Yep."

"And" — Gavin said, talking at a slow pace, trying to recount the convoluted nature of the story — "this same guy, Eli Bren, who's also Erin's dad, is the one who killed her mother back when she was a kid."

"Right," Ben nodded.

Gavin let out a puff of air.

"Yeah," Ben said, seconding Gavin's response.

Gavin looked up at Ben. "That's messed up," he said.

"Tell me about it," Ben said.

"How's Erin taking all of this?"

It was a moment before Ben spoke.

"I don't know," he said. "Honestly, I don't think she is yet. She's been going non-stop since Colombia. And I don't think it's really hit her. Not fully at least."

They were both quiet for another moment. And then Gavin spoke.

"What I don't get," he said. "Well—" he corrected himself "— there's a *lot* I don't get. But what still doesn't make sense is the part about Jonah Lennox. I mean, a few months ago, in Ghana, he and his monkey Keeler tried to kill you and Erin. And almost did. So why did he help you in Colombia?"

Ben got up and started to walk, pacing Erin's living room.

"I've thought about this, too," Ben said. "Quite a bit. It's like something changed there. I wouldn't have believed it myself, if I wasn't there. He's certainly still the same 'Jonah Lennox.' But…I dunno, there was something else there, too. Like, he'd found someone he hated even more, and he was willing to do anything to get to it. Including helping us."

"What do you mean?"

"I don't know," Ben said. "But he had plenty of chances to turn on us."

"But he shot, uh — what was his name?"

"Rafael."

"Right."

"I have a theory on that, too," Ben said. "I believe he did it so that Val wouldn't. It was a distraction. But it also kept him alive. He knew if she shot him, she'd definitely kill him."

"I don't know…," Gavin said.

"I know I know, it sounds crazy," Ben said. "But it's the only explanation that makes sense of everything."

"Is that what Erin thinks?" Gavin asked.

She'd been through a lot, Ben thought. She's just found out that the man who is her father is the same one who killed her mother. And now, asking her to believe that the guy who tried to kill us last year is just, now, on our team, like good 'ole buddies. It was a far reach. And he knew it.

"There's some stuff on Paul's list for you," Ben said, changing the subject.

"For me?" Gavin said.

"Yeah," Ben said. "Part of my instructions from Paul was to find you."

$$18$$

TAIL

E RIN HUNG UP THE PHONE WITH MCGILLIS. SHE TOLD
him the three-minute version of everything that had
happened since they'd last talked.

McGillis didn't trust Jonah, which made her feel a little
better. But then again, McGillis didn't trust anyone. He was
in the newspaper industry for a reason. But when she got to
the part about Eli Bren being her father, McGillis was quiet,
and for once, he didn't have anything to say about that. That
was curious to Erin. Maybe he was chewing on it. Or maybe
he was just didn't feel it was his place to comment. Though…
she wished he would. She needed this to all make sense.

She walked down First and crossed C Street, deciding to
not call a car for the ride back home. She'd walk a bit, think a
bit, then take the Metro the rest of the way.

The night was colder than she preferred. But the crisp air
had a clarifying factor to it. And she needed that right now.
She pulled her jacket tighter around her and pushing her
hands into her pockets.

She pulled out her phone to call Ben, but then she put it
back in again, remembering he'd gotten weird about phones

since getting Paul's letter. She knew what was coming, and that it wasn't completely unfounded. But she figured it was still too early for someone to be listening in.

Anyway, she'd see him shortly, and it would do her good to think through this on her own first. They had a plan to bring Eli Bren down. Finally. And now, with everything Paul had done when he was alive, the intel he'd provided, and, along with his posthumous guidance, they might actually be able to do this.

But getting that close, becoming *that* kind of a threat to a man like Eli Bren didn't come without its consequences or risks. And that's what Paul's guidelines were about.

She felt a twinge in her chest, thinking about Paul. It's almost like he was still with them. Using all of his work. Discovering all of his notes. Referring to him on a daily basis, like they could just call him up and talk to him. In his way, Paul had filled the missing role of father for her.

And then a strange thought occurred to her, one she hadn't previously thought about… she'd just learned that Eli Bren was her biological father. But she wondered if he knew she was.

She thought back to the last time she'd seen him, in his office on the top floor of his building in Bogotá. He'd said something. Asked her how old she was. It didn't mean anything to her at the time. But now…now that she knew who *he* was, she was wondering if he knew who she was. That she was his…daughter.

She kept walking. She was no longer in the manicured government area of the Dirksen building where she'd come from, but was now walking past NoMa, one of the D.C. art museums. It took up the better part of a block, though, at this time, on a Sunday, like most of the area, it was currently closed. She turned down L street, which was framed by tall office buildings. There was a car or two driving by, but it was mostly empty.

She walked on the sidewalk, stepping around a worker-less construction zone. She'd seen almost no one since she turned on this street. As she walked around the orange temporary fencing, she could hear her shoes crunching over the gravel and debris that spread out onto the rest of the street. It made a louder sound than she expected, echoing off the high buildings next to her. An eerie reminder of how empty the place was.

The wind blew from behind her. She walked a step faster and pulled her collar up closer. The wind started blowing the debris behind her, making it crunch, like when she walked over it. No, she thought, that wasn't right—

She stopped walking, involuntarily. The crunching sound. It stopped, too.

The wind blew again, hard. But still no sound.

She started walking again, listening as hard as she could for the sound to happen again. Nothing. She took a chance and looked over her shoulder. No one was there. She let out a breath she didn't know she was holding. Maybe it was just the wind after all. Or her imagination. These thoughts of conspiracy were beginning to weigh on her. To make her invent things.

She looked around as she kept walking, making a note of where she was.

Politics wasn't the only dangerous thing in D.C. The city had a crime problem. The smash-and-grab, stick-em-up kind of crime. And it'd been like this for as long as she could remember. But Erin knew how to take care of herself. And while she wasn't in a particularly bad area of the city, she was beginning to rethink the wisdom of her shortcut.

And her shoes…if it came to that.

She heard another sound. She looked back over her

shoulder in a passing glance. Probably just the wind. But just as a precaution—

But this time, in the second she looked over her shoulder — she saw someone.

She whipped her head back around and looked at the spot, where the movement was.

This time, there was no one.

Was her imagination making up things?

She stared at the spot where she'd seen the movement. It was in a deep shadow. But the wind wasn't blowing.

And then — there, *she saw it again.*

There was definitely someone there, in the shadow.

There were only a few reasons a person would be on this street at this time. But someone hiding in a shadow…

She turned around, and began stiffly walking as fast as she could. She forced herself to stay calm. Whatever this was, she could handle it *if she kept her cool.*

She was walking faster now. There was a small inlet between buildings, on her right. Without looking behind her, she darted down it. It was designed for delivery vehicles and it was lined with closed garages and service doors. Her brisk walk turned into a jog. She made it to the other side, which wasn't more than a walkway now, no longer wide enough for cars to fit through. She turned left and started walking, still fast. She looked up at a street sign. She was on Pierce street, walking parallel now to where she was a moment ago.

Pierce was a little bit darker. But she knew the Yellow Line of the Metro had a terminal a little bit away, maybe four or five blocks from here. That distance felt like miles. And it was a straight shot, with nothing behind her, meaning if someone was following her, as soon as they walked through the building cut-through she'd just taken, they'd immediately see her.

Across the street was a shop entrance with its metal cover pulled down over the front. She looked behind her, saw nothing, and darted across the street. She slipped into the shallow inlet and waited. This gave her a good view of where she'd just come from. And if someone was coming — following her — she'd see him.

Her heart was beating hard. As she assessed her situation, she realized this vantage point didn't do anything to hide her. She hoped it wouldn't come to that.

She waited, watching.

Nothing was happening.

She thought about Morocco. *How had Jonah found her?* she wondered. Paul had warned them this would happen. But it was all moving faster than she'd expected.

She pulled out her phone to call McGillis. He knew these streets and this city better than anyone she knew. It was just a safety measure. Most of her body was standing in the shadow of the closed garage. She'd get him on the phone, and at the very least, he could talk her down. And, at worse, well… She swiped open her phone. Its screen was bright. Her eyes had adjusted to the dark, and she had to squint. Then she looked down, she'd just painted herself in light. Her phone's light made her feel exposed.

She immediately looked back up, to the spot where she'd been a moment ago. To the spot where, if someone was following her, he'd have to pass through.

As she did, she thought she saw some movement stop.

She froze, holding the phone tight against her jacket.

She'd stopped breathing.

She couldn't see anything else. *Why had she taken her eyes off the spot?* She thought she might throw up from how much her heart was rocking her chest.

She looked hard at the spot, where she'd seen the latest

movement. It was just beyond the alleyway entrance, near a parked car.

She kept her eyes trained on the spot, determined to wait it out. The wind gusted. No movement. How long had she been staring at that spot? She had no concept of time right now. Her eyes were still trained on the spot, holding her phone to her body. Still no movement. Maybe she really was seeing things. Or the wind was playing tricks on her. Probably. It had been a *very* long week.

Her shoulders relaxed a little, and as she pulled her phone back out, still not taking her eyes off the spot.

No, it was something. She saw it again. *The movement.*

A person. It was a person. And he just darted between cars.

There was no doubt now.

Someone was definitely there. *Following her.*

Her insides sunk, as she realized her gut had been right on this one.

And, with that, her panic was back, raging to take her down. She was doing her best not to lose that battle. Pushing it all down, keeping control as best she could.

She was going to have to make a move for it. There was no other choice.

She couldn't see him. But she saw where he was.

The car he was behind, it was next to a line of parked cars. From the angle she was at, he may be able to move a few car-lengths forward, closer to her, without her being able to see him.

That was it.

If she didn't move now, she might not be able to.

She kept her eyes focused on where she last saw his form. And then, she saw it again. Movement, between cars. She swore silently under her breath.

He was moving. Closer to her. And he'd be parallel to her very soon — with only a quiet empty street between them.

Erin reached down and pulled off her shoes. The cement was like ice. It gave her a burst of focus. She was going to double-back. She gave herself one more second to watch the spot — where the man had been, behind the lines of cars.

And then, she stepped out and ran as fast as she could.

19

THE MAN

ERIN WAS RUNNING FLAT OUT NOW, SHOES IN HAND. She was headed back up Pierce, on the opposite side she came down before. The man was behind her, running. She could clearly hear his heavy footfalls on the pavement, and his breath, panting close behind her. The street was stupidly quiet. No one to flag down, no one to call out to for help.

Erin was fast — faster than most. And that small amount of control helped her keep her panic under wraps, just enough to keep going.

But she knew she couldn't keep this up for much longer. Especially not barefoot.

She pushed herself, harder, on the balls of her feet, her shoes slapping her hand, as she ran. Her own breath coming harder now.

She felt like she might be widening the gap — but she couldn't risk turning to look. She took a deep breath, concentrating on the sounds coming from behind her. Still there. The man was still running, full out, after her. And he sounded close. The gap between her and him wasn't as big as she'd hoped.

Up ahead, she saw another service area, for delivery trucks, carved in between buildings. She pushed harder and sprinted for it. Once in, she'd dash down it. Add in as many turns and corners that she could — removing as many direct lines-of-sites as she could. She prepared to cut hard, to the left, slowing a tiny bit so that she could lean into the turn and keep as much momentum as possible. Then, as she neared, on purpose she almost passed the opening, — partly to give her pursuer the smallest amount of reaction time, to correct his own course — and also to use the opposite wall to push off of in her turn.

She did it. She made the turn.

But this cut-through wasn't like the one she'd gone through before.

It wasn't a cut-through at all.

No... she thought.

A dead end.

She immediately stopped, inhaling, trying to catch her breath. She turned around, as quickly as she'd run in. She'd dart back out, straight across the street, hopefully throw him off of her intent—

But as soon as she started to move, he was already there, blocking her way.

He was a big man. And she was genuinely surprised he'd kept up with her as well as he had. The light from the streetlight was flooding the inlet. But it was coming in from the outside of the area, from the street. And it was backlighting his form, keeping his face in shadows.

Erin didn't move. She could see his shoulders rising and falling, catching his breath.

"What—" she started, but her throat closed, choking the words from coming out. She tried to clear her throat, but it was dry and the attempt was useless. She tried again, pushing the words out more like a whisper than anything else.

"What do you want," she said finally.

He took another step forward. Not bothering to answer her.

The inlet was only about twelve feet deep, and maybe that wide. When Erin darted in, she covered most of that distance just by not stopping. And now, she realized, she was trapped.

Behind her, off to one side was a dumpster. She took another step back, putting as much distance between her and the over-sized man as she could. As she did, she knocked into the dumpster, it's corner jabbing her ribs from behind. The metal corner of the dumpster hurt, forcing her to move farther into the space between the wall and dumpster. If she stretched out her hands, she could touch the dumpster and the wall. No more room to move.

The man took two more steps, both toward her. He'd not completely blocked her.

She stepped back again, this time bumping into the brick wall behind her. It almost seemed to push back on her as she touched it. Like everything inside was moving in on her. She leaned against it, putting her weight into it. As if the extra millimeters of space would somehow make a difference.

"Who…who are you," she called out, finding her voice.

The man didn't respond. He just took another step, this one, more casual than it should have been. He was about six feet away now, almost close enough to touch her. But now, she could see his face, lit from a small light off to the side.

The light… She looked to her right. It was a small light over a gray service door. The doorknob opened closest to her. And the handle was about a third of the distance between her and him. In her favor.

She lunged for the handle, preparing to open It, and use the frame to pull herself in, slamming it behind her. At the very least it would buy her a few more seconds lead and a chance to move again.

But... on the other side of her lunge, she'd landed at the door already. Only, when she turned the handle, nothing happened. She rattled it. Still nothing.

It was locked.

She swore loudly at this, pushing herself back against the wall.

The man laughed as he took another step toward her. The light over the door, that had just let her down, was still showering his face.

Then, as if he'd decided he had enough messing around, his smile faded, and he took a few more steps, closing the distance between them almost instantly. She was now standing with the brick wall on one side, the dumpster on the other, and the entire bulk of this man, just eighteen inches away from her.

She was completely pinned.

She looked up at him. But his entire front was now cast in shadow. She could see nothing of him or his face. Erin was doing her best to keep her eyes open. To not shut down. She could hear his breathing. He was still breathing heavily. But it wasn't the kind of heavy that came from the cardio workout she'd just given him.

Erin glanced around, looking desperately for any escape hatch she'd missed. The man was at least three feet wide, and at this distance — closer than an arm's length — he might as well have been a hundred feet wide. She looked back into the darkness where his face was.

Then, with unexpected speed, he lifted his hand and struck — no pushed — her forehead back, pressing the back of her head into the brick wall behind her. He held her head there, pinned back, one hand covering one of her eyes in the process. She felt his rough sweaty hand on her face, and she felt as though she might throw up.

At this angle, his face turned slightly, and she could see an ugly twisted smile. Like *this* was his payment. She twisted to kick, straight up the middle. But he grabbed her arm, like he knew the move was coming, and shifted her balance in the process, causing her kick to go nowhere.

He shook his head, slowly. He was playing with her.

He was tall, and his chin was just above her eye line. He moved his body closer to her, almost *on* her. She could still see his eyes looking down at her. And then, his eyes darted down the length of her body, before coming back to her face, not making eye contact, but watching her mouth. Her heart thumped so hard she thought it might stop.

And then, his dirty smile twisted into something grotesque. He was still holding her — one hand on her forehead, pressing her against the wall, with the other holding her arm firmly. His grip didn't relax, but she felt a twitch run through him. And his eyes, they seemed to refocus — as if she was no longer the object of his thoughts.

He opened his mouth. To say something. But he only let out a small cough.

And then, he moved lower, down her front. She tried one last effort, to push him off of her. Knowing it wouldn't work. Something inside wouldn't let her give up. Couldn't just *let* this happen.

But, then, something *did* happen.

Her push…it *worked*.

She pushed harder, and he backed off. He took his hand off her head, dropping it down to his side. He was looking just past her face now, to the brick behind her. Like he was struggling to remember something. But he was still holding her arm tightly.

She reached out and pushed him a third time, and he

moved back. This time, dropping to his knees. His eyes were no longer focused on anything. And his breath, it was coming in a different kind of rhythm. More of a gasp.

She yanked her arm, breaking it out of his grip. As she did it, he twisted, falling over. A part of his body collapsed onto her feet, almost knocking her over. For the first time, she took her eyes off of him and looked up.

She — they — weren't alone.

Another man was standing there. But he was in the same shadow this man had been in. Though, his frame was smaller. He was about five feet away.

Erin's eyes instinctively darted back to the man still laying on her feet.

And that's when she noticed, the knife sticking out of the big man's back. His body twitched, but was otherwise still.

He was dead.

She looked back up, still feeling the dead man's weight on her feet. Still nowhere else to go. Still not out of this…

The new man, though — the one who just killed the big man — took a step forward. The light slid onto his face as he moved, and for the first time, Erin saw who it was.

Jonah Lennox.

20

THE SKY

"*YOU*," ERIN CALLED OUT.

There was only fury in her now. Whatever trepidation or anxiety she'd felt before had now been replaced with rage. She wanted to say more. To let the rest of it pour out of her — the questions and accusations — all in one damning cascade.

But she didn't. She just stood there. Waiting.

"Thank you," Jonah said.

Of everything she'd expected him to say, this was not on the list.

"Thank you?" she repeated.

"Yes," he said, taking a step forward. "That's usually what people in *your* position say to someone in *my* position."

She looked down at the large dead man. He was still. And his arm and shoulder were laying over her feet. She pulled herself out from under the man's bulk, and reached down to pick up her shoe. She glanced around for the other one, not wanting to take her eyes off Jonah for longer than she had to. She found her other shoe, wedged under the man's body. She pushed him, tentatively, grabbed her missing shoe, and let the rest of his dead weight fall back in place.

Erin slipped her shoes back on and stepped to the side, keeping an eye on Jonah the whole time. For his part, he seemed content to watch her maneuver. As she moved around the body, she almost slipped as she accidentally stepped on one of his fingers. She winced, not looking down. Erin moved back against the wall, where the door was, keeping as much distances between her and Jonah as she could.

He walked forward, but not to her. He knelt down by the man and pulled his knife out of the man's back. It made a sick sliding noise as it came out, and his body shook a slight bit, as if the muscles were still holding onto the knife. There wasn't much blood. He wiped the blade on the man's clothes and put it away.

Jonah stood back up and turned away from her. As if, after all that, he was just going to leave.

"Wait," she said. And, to her amazement, he did. He turned his head, listening. "Morocco," she said. "You were there. You tried to get into Paul's safe room. I saw you. On the camer—"

"Shhh," he hissed. He looked around. But not at her. He held out a hand for her to be quiet, like he was listening for something else.

But there was no one else here. And, other than distant traffic sounds, the only thing she *did* notice was a faint hum, from above, on the building or something. It wasn't remarkable. It sounded like an air condition vent or fan. But Jonah was still, not looking at her.

Erin broke the silence.

"What?" she said.

He held up a finger, motioning for her to wait.

Erin had next to no patience for Jonah and power plays.

And now, she was hardly in a mood to put up with this. "Either you tell me what's—," she said, but he cut her off with a look, and she stopped herself.

He was looking at her directly now. And his face, was… different. Something about it caught her off guard.

"Stop talking," he mouthed to her.

Then he looked up. He was looking for something. Erin looked up too, keeping one eye on him. Honestly, at this point, she didn't know what to think. He appeared to be looking for something. But there was nothing *up* there. The city's light pollution meant it left nothing up there but just a dark sky. No clouds, no stars. Just darkness. A small swarm of insects was circling the streetlight off to the side, buzzing and slapping the glass covering the bulb.

Jonah, still looking up, cautiously walked over to where she was. She was still standing against the wall. As he moved, she watched him. He came within a few inches of her, and she felt herself instinctively move back against the wall.

He held a finger to his lips, and looked her in the eye. She'd never been *this* close to him. His face was lit by the small light over her shoulder, the one over the service door she'd tried to escape through a moment ago. And, for the first time, she saw wrinkles. Stress marks on his face. The cool facade that he'd always shown the world, at this distance, looked, more…normal.

"Not here," he mouthed to her.

He looked up again. She glanced up again, too. Something about the way he was acting…it didn't feel like a game, even one he would play.

"I'll explain everything," he said, looking back at her, still whispering. "But not here."

21

SENATOR AVERY CLEASON

SENATOR AVERY CLEASON HAD BEEN HAVING A BAD DAY. No, make that: a bad week might be more accurate.

Success in Washington was about having the right perceptions and the right allies. And the number one rule for survival? *Make the right friends.* Cleason was beginning to realize he might have misjudged one of those friends. In a big way. And now he was working through that.

Eli Bren had been a longtime buddy. They'd served together. Granted, that had been the result of the draft. Not exactly patriotism. But even then, he should have seen it in Bren. The signs were there. Cleason, for his part, didn't always agree with everything his government did. And Vietnam was one big case study in bad decisions. But Bren — he was different. He was… dissident. Though, in a quiet way. Which, in some ways, should have raised more alarm bells than it did.

But the two of them had had some fun over the years, too. Eli Bren and Avery Cleason had the special kind of relationship that you only get from living a life, parallel to one another, over decades. It wasn't friendly in the normal sense of the word. But it was deep. Or, at least, mutual.

And so Cleason had pushed for Eli to get the Defense contract; the one Cleason's committee oversaw. And, in truth, he believed Eli would be the best man for the job. Over the years, Eli had developed a powerful empire and network of resources. He'd do it right. And, ultimately, Cleason believed this would be a benefit to their country.

And of course, that was all before…

This, what he was looking at now… he shook his head. He had the photos and other document scans that Erin Reed, the journalist, had sent him, spread out over his desk. How had she gotten this? he wondered. He wished, earlier this evening, that he'd been able to meet with her. But he was having to do damage control on several other fronts. This Eli Bren stuff was very close to blowing up. And if the winds blew in the direction they were threatening, it could very well take him down with Bren…

He picked up his phone to call Amy, his assistant. To reschedule with Ms. Reed. Even tonight would work, if Amy could get her. The rule between Cleason and Amy was that when he was working, she was. He knew that presented challenges for her, personally. But she was invaluable to him. And he always tried to make it up to her.

Which is why it was strange that she wasn't answering. She *always* answered. Cleason looked down at his desk phone. None of the lights were lit, so she wasn't on the other line. He lifted himself out of his chair, to walk to the outer office. Maybe she'd stepped away, he thought.

Then, as he was getting up, his door opened.

He let his weight sink back into his chair without looking up.

"Amy," he said, "can you get the journalist, Erin Reed,

back here." He glanced at his watch again. "Tonight if…" he stopped talking as he looked up.

It wasn't Amy.

Before him was a slender woman with dark shoulder-length hair, dressed in business attire — a light blouse and dark skirt. For the briefest moment, he thought it *was* Erin Reed, but he'd seen her picture in the media, and this wasn't her.

Something was holding him back from talking. This had never happened before. Amy was an excellent gatekeeper. And Derek beyond her… How was this woman now standing in front of him? Maybe she was a lobbyist. There was no end to those people's determination…

She stood there, watching him.

"Who are you?" he said finally. And *What are you doing here?* he wanted to ask, along with about a dozen other questions.

She didn't answer him, but instead began walking toward him.

She swayed when she walked. Maybe more than she needed it. Something about this made Cleason think about his wife. But not in a guilty kind of way. They had a good relationship. They were high school sweethearts, and they'd been together ever since. Even through the war years. But after years and years of marriage, it had come to feel more like a business. Or a routine. And that was… still okay. Both of them had settled into it, and found a way to make it work. They each had developed their own circles and ways of life to deal with the distance. But, that didn't mean he didn't, some-times, need… well…

She kept walking toward him. She passed the double couches, walking between them, toward his desk.

"You with Detroit?" he said.

It wasn't unlike some lobbyists — big ones, like the auto

industry — to send a woman like this. 'Companionship' went a long way in getting what you want. And as much as he fought against stuff like this in the public arena, he knew all too well: it worked.

"No," she said.

Her accent, he thought… It sounded Spanish. Maybe. *How old was she?* he wondered. As she got closer, he couldn't be sure, but he didn't think this was *that* kind of thing. She was four feet away from him now. And she stopped and stood just across his desk.

"Who then?" he said.

She leaned down, resting her palms on the paperwork he had scattered and leaned forward.

"A friend," she said.

Fun and games were one thing. A little bit of *stress-relief* could go a long way. But there were some basics he had to get out of the way first. She stood up and walked around his long desk. Slowly. As she did, she took her eyes off of him. But he didn't take his off of her.

"Who?" he said. "And how did you get in here?"

She turned at the edge of his desk and walked closer to him. Now there was nothing between him and her. As she'd been walking, he'd been swiveling his chair, turning it inch by inch, to follow her arc. And then, another thought occurred to him… "Where's Amy?" he said. One of her greatest skills was her discretion. But this, this wasn't right — she didn't just let people in…

He stood up out of his chair, to go investigate. Cleason turned and walked around the opposite side of his desk, away from the woman.

"I sent her away," the woman said. Her accent, definitely Spanish.

Cleason stopped and turned back around. The woman was standing behind his desk on one side, and Cleason stood on the other side. Now the only thing between them was his chair, still slowly twisting from him just getting out of it a few seconds ago. He faced her full and began walking back to her, pushed the chair out of his way.

"Who are you with?" he demanded.

"Eli Bren," she said softly. "He asked me to… come see you."

"Why?"

She walked the rest of the distance to him. All pretense gone. She was standing right in front of him now. Cleason was not a tall man. But he was still a good six inches taller than her. She was standing less than a foot away from him. As if waiting for *him* to make the next move. But if there was anything he'd learned in his decades of public service, it was that entrapment is a real thing.

He talked, quieter now.

"What's your name?"

"Val," she said.

"Val," he said, "why are you here?"

Her eyes were dark brown. And they were barreling into his. Without looking away, she pulled the chair back in place.

"Sit?" she said.

He did.

She unbuttoned her top button.

He was uncomfortable with this. Not *this*. But having her so close to… He involuntarily glanced back at his desk. He had classified papers, open and on his desk two feet away from them. And if the right person had access to his office — normally, he kept secure stuff in the safe. But that was open, too. He hadn't expected any visitors. He'd been in the middle of something, and…

She was closer to him now. Almost on top of him. He was having a hard time keeping his thoughts on anything else. She touched him. But, then, she pulled back, standing up again.

He let out a breath, trying not to betray anything.

"Drink?" she said.

"What?" he said. "Uh, yeah," he said, taking a moment. She'd already moved to the cabinet behind his desk and opened it, uncorking a crystal container and pouring a couple glasses. It was curious, how fast she found his stash. It wasn't exactly visible to visitors. It was as if she was already familiar with his office…

As she bent, to put the bottle back, he noticed the zipper above her skirt was down, but just an inch. He should have used the delay to get up and close his safe, to put the classified stuff back in it. But, to be honest, he was having a hard time thinking of anything *but* her right now.

She turned back around, holding both drinks. She didn't smile. Didn't seem like the friendly type. But, he through with a touch of humor, she wasn't really relying on *those* assets right now. He took the glass. They both drank. She drank all of hers in one drink. He sipped his. He chuckled. "There's no need to rush *everything*," he said.

She put her empty glass back down on his desk.

He opened his mouth to say something else, but he was having a hard time getting it out. His mouth was dry. More than usual. Bourbon — good Bourbon — didn't normally have that effect on him. He cleared his throat again. Her empty glass was on his desk. He was having trouble focusing on it. His own glass was in his hand. But it almost slipped out. He looked down at it. It, too, was a little bit blurry.

Val reached down and took the glass out of his hand. She set it next to hers. Then, she began to unbutton his shirt. She even tore it a little bit. One of the buttons, he noticed, popped off. But his mind wasn't on that. As beautiful as she was, his mind was on something else he'd just discovered. His throat. He felt like he was having an allergic reaction. And his heart rate, it was through the roof. He tried to stand, but she pushed him back down into his chair.

He opened his mouth to protest. To tell her that he needed help. That something was wrong.

She touched his lips, signaling for him to be quiet.

She leaned down into his ear.

"I've poisoned you," she said.

His body jerked. He was having a hard time moving his arms. He felt like he was sliding out of his chair. No, not *felt*. He couldn't *feel* anything. There was a sensation pulsing through his body. A euphoric wave of nothingness. He wanted to ask her what she wanted. What he needed to do now. But it was becoming hard to even breathe.

Though, strangely, his heart rate was slowing down now.

"What have you done?" he wanted to say. But it was only a thought. His lips didn't even open. Or try to. They weren't his anymore. He couldn't see her face anymore either. Just a blurry white area that used to be her shirt.

And then, he laid down, surprised how comfortable his office chair was. He was ready for a long, deep sleep. One he needed more than anything else right now...

Avery Cleason closed his eyes, and then, like that, he was gone.

22

MEG'S DINER

Erin sat across the table from Jonah in an open-all-night diner. It wasn't a far walk from where they'd been. Jonah had walked to the diner like he was familiar with it. Or maybe he'd seen it on his way. It was only a few blocks.

On the walk over, neither of them talked. Erin, for her part, gave Jonah some space, letting him walk ahead of her. Mostly, she did it to keep an eye on him. He would occasionally look over his shoulder — through her. Or up in the sky.

"What do you keep looking up for?" she finally asked him.

But he didn't answer, just kept walking forward.

He opened the diner door, without waiting for her, and walked to the back. Since arriving, neither of them had ordered anything. They were sitting in a booth, near the back, away from the windows. Erin watched him from across the table. Jonah sat still, waiting. Then he looked at her in the pointed way that she felt was so condescending.

"Well?" he said finally.

"Morocco," she said.

"What about it?"

"Why were you there?"

"Same reason you were."

That was a non-answer. Not to mention, she wasn't sure that was true. How much did he know about the information Paul had collected… Did he even know what Paul had done?

"Tell me," she said.

Jonah blinked.

"Paul had been amassing intel on Eli. Damning intel. And he kept it in a safe room in Tangier, guarded by the more-loyal-than-competent shop owner by the name of Sabeer."

Erin thought that last part was a bit unfair.

"How did you know about the intel Paul had gathered?" Erin said.

"An involuntary tip-off," Jonah said. "From Val," he added.

"Val? How did *she* know?"

"Probably from you."

"What?"

Jonah leaned forward, resting his forearms on the table. "Why did they let you live?" he said. "In Bogotá."

That was a question Erin had started to wonder herself. At first, she didn't think anything of it. They'd killed Paul. They *thought* Rafael was dead. She'd sort of figured that was enough. As if they'd made their point. But, the more she thought about it, the less sense that made. If they wanted to cover their tracks, leaving Erin alive was a loose end.

Erin knew, once they started Paul's plan — his Vesper Protocol as he called it — that they'd have people on them. They'd need to go off-grid. But, she was realizing she'd been naive to not realize they were *already* on to her. Already watching her.

She decided not to answer Jonah's question. Not to let him drive this.

"So you were going to…what?" she said. "Beat Eli and Val to the punch and take Paul's intel for yourself?"

"No," he said. He turned away, watching something out of Erin's field of view. But she didn't take her eyes off of him.

"No?"

"Believe it or not," he said. "I wasn't there for Paul's secret stash. I was there because I knew *you* were."

"Me?"

"Your friend, Sabeer, he was sloppy."

Erin opened her mouth to respond, but he cut her off.

"The man Val sent to find and recover Paul's files on Eli," he continued. "It didn't take him long to find you two. I was already following him. So I just waited."

"Waited…for what?"

"For him to make his move. He followed your friend down into the tunnels under his shop. Now that the location of Paul's storeroom was known and exposed, it would have been easy for a pro to come in and take it."

"But *you* were the one on the video…," Erin said.

Erin saw a little smile curl at his lips. "The video," he said to himself, as he let out a little puff of air. "Clearly, it helped."

He was teasing her. Clearly it *hadn't*, he meant, as they hadn't seen the other man.

"Prove it," she said.

"Prove what?"

"Prove that you weren't alone."

"Where you watching the cameras the entire time?"

Now it was Erin's turn to look away.

"Right," he said. "Anyway, why would I be lying about that?"

"So then what happened to him? The one you were following?"

"I killed him," he said, standing up.

"Wait," Erin said, standing with him. "Where are you going?"

He paused, and moved his head toward the restroom, while keeping his eyes on her.

"That okay with you?"

She sat back down, not answering, while he walked off to the bathroom. She watched him, making sure that was really where he went. She stared at the restroom door for a long moment. Then she thought again about the man, where they'd just come from. The one who, she knew, was going to do something bad. The same one who Jonah had just killed… for her.

He walked back to the table but didn't sit. She didn't stand.

"I have more questions," she said.

"Of course you do," he said with a sigh and sat.

"So, let me get this straight," she said. "You knew I was in Morocco, because *Val* figured it out. And she sent someone, to follow me, and get Paul's intel on Eli Bren. But you found him first. And killed him."

He watched her, without changing his expression.

"But what about tonight?" she said. "Had someone been following me?" Erin wasn't trained in counter-surveillance. She was a journalist. But she knew people. And she knew when things were wrong. She was having a hard time believing someone had been following her since Morocco.

"Tonight," he said. "That was something else."

"What do you mean?"

"When you sent those images to Cleason, you started something."

"Are you saying that man wasn't from Eli Bren?"

Jonah was quiet for another long moment.

"I'm saying, I don't know," he said. "There are more people than just Eli Bren interested in Eli Bren's success."

Erin was quiet, watching him. Jonah pulled both of his hands up to his mouth, and was silent while he looked out at nothing. Erin broke the silence.

"Why did you do it?" she said.

It took him a moment to look at her, like he was stuck in his own thoughts, far away.

"Do what?" he said.

"All of it. Why did you bother to come to Morocco? Or here now? The guy…tonight." She felt like she should thank him. He did, after all, just save her life. But she was having a hard time bringing herself to that. "Why?" she finished.

Jonah looked back to the door, over her shoulder. It was another long moment before he said anything. She watched his face the entire time. He wasn't tense. Or cold. But Erin though she picked up the faintest bit of sadness. Like she was seeing something she shouldn't be seeing right now. And then, in a moment, whatever that look was, it had gone. His eyes locked back onto hers. He was himself again.

When he spoke, it was slow, and measured.

"I did it," he said. "Because I found out who you were."

Erin sat, watching him, giving him room to talk.

He let out a low sigh. "I figured it out sometime back," he said. "But it was only just recently, that I'd been able to confirm it. When I…," he trailed off.

Erin looked around. The bell behind them, over the entrance to the diner, dinged. Two college kids walked in and sat on the other side of the diner. She looked back at Jonah.

"When you what?" she prompted.

"When I decided he'd done enough," he said with a tone of finality.

"I don't understand what that means," she said.

He closed his eyes and opened them again, like he was blinking in slow motion. His eyes locked on to hers again. He wasn't talking. Like he was weighing the next part. Considering whether he should try to explain, or just stop about it altogether.

"Tell me," she said.

"There's a lot you don't know," he started. "A lot that will…change things."

"Okay," she said, noticing her own voice softening. As if to help him along. She thought about the absurdity of that. Her coaxing Jonah Lennox along. She almost felt like she was out of her body, watching from afar, as she and Jonah had this conversation. It was surreal.

"We…," he said, after another long pause.

She nodded.

"You and I," he started again. "We share the same father."

23

LOVEBIRDS

WHATEVER ERIN HAD BEEN EXPECTING JONAH TO SAY — it wasn't this. At first, the words just seemed to bounce off of her. What he'd said. *Who* he'd said he was. It was like someone reached up and pulled a mask off of their face, exposing themself as a grotesque and goofy alien. It wasn't real. It couldn't be. It was just too strange, too unexpected.

It was another moment before she realized Jonah was still talking. But she hadn't heard a word of it.

"Can you—" she said. "Can you just stop for a minute."

She looked down at the table, but not really looking at it. Her hands were on the tabletop, her fingers spread out. Like she was doing everything to hold on. She took a deep breath and then looked back at him. "How can that even be *remotely* true?" she said finally.

He was calm. And for his part, taking this much better than she was.

"Let's start here," he said. "Do you know *who* our father is?"

She was feeling trapped now. Not because of Jonah. But because this, here, now, was forcing her to deal with something that she was only just realizing she'd never properly unpacked yet. She hadn't yet dealt with the pain and confusion that came with knowing *Eli Bren* was her biological father. Granted, she'd been going almost non-stop since she'd found out. And all of that came immediately after the events down in Bogotá. What he'd done to Paul... someone who was more of an *actual* father than Bren could ever be. After Erin's mother died, she was sent to a therapist. And she remembered her therapist telling her about grief. Grief wasn't just crying and being sad. There were other parts, like denial and bargaining. And, here now, sitting with Jonah Lennox of all people, after someone had just tried to kill her, she realized she was smack in the middle of one of these grief stages. Grief for the fact that her father was really Eli Bren.

She looked at Jonah again. And in a quiet calm voice — one that didn't sound like her right now — she answered him. "Yes," she said.

"Okay," he said. "And do you know how?"

The truth was, yes, she knew that too. Thanks to Paul. Her mother, Gillian, she knew her mother had had a fling with Bren. When she was young. In her twenties.

Erin nodded her head in response.

"What you don't know," he said. "Is *why* he had an affair with...," he almost didn't say her name. "—with Gillian."

She listened, not blinking.

"It started with Lillian," he said.

"Lillian?"

"Lillian Lennox," he said the name with a softness that Erin had never heard — never imaged — could come from a person like Jonah Lennox. "She was my mother. She died that same year Bren and your mother were having an affair. Cancer. But they'd already become estranged. I was only twelve. But I hardly knew Eli. He wasn't exactly the father type," Jonah said.

The more the subject turned to Eli, the more his words dripped with disgust. And cold hate. "I only saw him a few times before she died. And then, after she was really sick, he visited. Only once. He could have done something. Could have paid for the right doctors. Or at least made her more comfortable. He'd become quite successful by then. He…"

Jonah turned away and stopped talking. He seemed to be more absorbed with his own pain and memories now, forgetting that he'd started this by explaining the gaps to Erin.

At the same time, Erin was beginning to understand how there could be someone else in the world who is actually *like* her. Well, not like her in the normal sense. She and Jonah still had almost nothing in common. But he… he'd been shaped like she was. Both of their mothers, taken too soon. And, in a weird way, the same person was responsible. Or maybe. Maybe Lillian would have died anyway. But…

Her thoughts were interrupted by a third voice. One clad in a blue apron and standing menacingly over the end of their tables.

"You love birds gonna sit here all night, or ya gonna order something?"

Erin looked up to see a largish woman who'd spoken. Her name tag read MEG.

"I'm sorry?" Erin said, not yet understanding her words.

The woman was looking down at the two of them. Her weight was propped on one leg, like she'd done her part, and it was clearly their turn to reciprocate.

"I don't run a charity here," she said.

Food, Erin realized. She started to look at her watch. How long had they been here, she wondered. She reached for a menu, though she wasn't remotely hungry. In fact, the image of putting food in her mouth right now made her feel more like throwing up. Her hands moved on autopilot.

"No," Jonah said. He didn't look up at the woman, but instead waving a hand, to shoo her.

"Listen—" she started, raising a finger.

Erin looked up at her, with a smile. "Just a coffee," she said kindly.

Meg pulled back the daggers she'd been sending Jonah's way and looked at Erin, suspiciously.

"A coffee?" she said. "That it?"

"Yes," Erin said. "For now," she added.

The woman, Meg, walked away without saying anything else. She looked both annoyed and defeated. A typical reaction, Erin had learned, that people felt after experiencing Jonah. In a few seconds she was back with a single white glass mug. She set it in front of Erin and sloshed black coffee into it.

"Thanks," Erin said. But the woman had already walked away.

Erin looked back at Jonah and blinked.

"So," she started. "Does this... I mean— Does this make us... *siblings?*"

24

WORST CASE SCENARIO

"Outside of Cain," Ben said. "Jonah has to be the worst big brother in the history of…," he trailed off, thinking.

"People?" Gavin suggested.

Ben thought about that. "Yeah, that sounds about right."

Erin didn't sleep much last night. After she and Jonah finished talking — and after three more cups of coffee — they left. Jonah said he'd be in touch. She wasn't sure what that meant. And in a move that felt much closer to the reality she knew than the last few hours did, he didn't bother to walk her home. That, she felt, would have been a bridge too far — for both of them. She took the Metro home. And, other than her own hyperactive thoughts, the rest of the night was uneventful.

It was early morning, well before dawn, when she opened her front door. Ben, she noticed, was sleeping on the couch. And Gavin was in a sleeping bag on the living room floor. She made a mental note to clean out her home office tomorrow, assuming this would be their base of operations. At least she could give them a proper place to sleep, she thought. She went upstairs, thinking she'd fall quickly into a deep and needed sleep. But she didn't. Her brain wouldn't shut off. It kept replaying the man's face, then his dead body at her feet, then the strange conversation she'd had with Jonah.

The next morning, she told Ben and Gavin what happened the night before. But as she still felt like she was *in* the night before, having not really slept since then, she wasn't sure how coherent her story was. The main difference between last night and now was that now, she was tired. The adrenaline that had been propping her up earlier had long since left her system.

Ben walked into her kitchen and came back with a cup of coffee. He handed it to her.

"Thanks," she said. She put her hands around the hot cup, letting it warm her up. "The thing is," she said. "Yes, you're right. Jonah Lennox *is* a terrible person." The mental list she carried around, that validated that claim was a long and immediate one. "But, I think," she continued. "There's a reason for it."

Ben and Gavin sat, letting her talk.

"I know," she said, "that everyone is responsible for what they do. But hearing him last night... it's like, I could see into his past. What it was like having your mother abandoned by your father. And then, when she needed him most, left to die. All the while, being a helpless twelve-year-old. And then, as if that wasn't enough, being raised by that same father. Who," she added, "clearly didn't care for him enough to be a real father."

The two of them were silent.

Erin didn't look at either of them. She wasn't sure how good of a job she was doing at convincing them.

"It sucks the worst for kids," she said. "These kinds of things... it changes them." She was talking quieter now.

Trying not to project too much of her own loss and struggle into his story. "Anyway…"

She looked up at them. And they were both still sitting, watching her.

"You sure you're okay?" Ben said. "I mean…because."

"I know," she said. "And yes," she smiled. "Or I will be. Anyway, right now, we've got work to do."

Gavin reached over and grabbed his laptop.

Erin turned to Ben. "I'm going to reach out to Cleason first thing this morning. Just go there and wait until I can see him. Even if it takes all day."

"I dunno," Ben said. "Maybe that's not such a good idea. I mean, considering, you know, last night and all."

Erin was sitting in a chair, she leaned forward, still holding her coffee, letting the steam rise to her face.

"Yeah," she said, thinking. "But we've got to make contact. We've got to do something. And I need to see where he is in all of this. If he's going to be an ally or not."

Ben stood up and started pacing her living room. "Right…," he said. But she could tell he wasn't sure if that justified the risk.

"And time is going to be short," she said. "Last night showed us that."

"It also showed us," Ben said, "that we need to be more careful."

Erin knew this, too. If they — whoever they were — had sent someone to *kill* her, then they'd certainly be able to track them digitally — and probably, already were. Meaning, the next meeting with Cleason had to be in person. As Erin and Ben talked through this, Gavin was quiet, sitting off to the side next to Erin's phone on the couch, clicking away on his laptop.

"Maybe if we can get him a letter," Ben said. "Old

school. I can drop it off. Tell him: Meet us in a safe place…
or something."

"It'd never get through the filter in time," Erin said.

"Um, guys?" Gavin said, still looking at his laptop.

"Or maybe, I could go in as a journalist," Ben said, still
spitballing ideas. "About something urgent and…"

"I hear what you're saying," Erin said. "But that list is
well vetted. Besides, everyone with a blog and an opinion is a
'journalist' when they want to talk to someone like that."

"Guys," Gavin said again, louder this time.

Erin looked up and Ben stopped pacing.

Gavin stood up and turned his laptop around so they
could see the screen. He reached around and tapped a
button. The video went full screen and the sound came on. It
was a reporter, standing in front of the Dirksen Senate office
building — Senator Cleason's building. The same place Erin
had been a few hours earlier. There was a red "breaking"
banner in the corner of the screen.

Erin and Ben watched. An un-calm silence took over the
three of them, with only the news reporter's voice filling her
living room.

"Looks like," Gavin said. "We might have a much *bigger*
problem."

25

BREAKING NEWS

WASHINGTON DC — Senator Avery Cleason was found dead last night in his Dirksen building office. The cause for death is still unknown, but the FBI investigators believe faul play may be the cause.

The FBI has not released any official suspects, but a still-frame from a video camera was obtained. It shows the back of an unidentified woman (pictured). She was wearing a dark coat and has dark medium-length hair.

She was seen leaving the Dirksen building during the window the medical examiner believes Senator Cleason's death occurred. So far, she has not been identified. And the Dirksen Building staff does not have any record of her identity.

If you have any information or if you know the identify of this woman, use our hotline.

More details as the story unfolds.

26

TIGHTER

"So," Erin said, knocking on the door. "What did he say?"

Ben looked at her and shrugged. "He's...," he started. "It's complicated."

After Erin, Ben, and Gavin watched the breaking news about Senator Cleason, they switched into high gear. Whatever was going on, they didn't yet know all the behind the scenes players. And Jonah had hinted that there were more than just Eli Bren. Or, at least, Bren had a healthy network of resources supporting him.

But now, with Senator Cleason showing up dead — *murdered,* by the looks of it. It was one thing to send someone after Erin. She was, effectively, a nobody. But a United States Senator. Things had changed. And this was bigger than any of them thought.

Immediately after they watched the press briefing, Ben wondered out loud if it was the same guy who went after Erin. "The timing would make sense," he said. That was true, Erin thought. Not to mention, convenient for them, as

Jonah had just killed that guy. The threat wouldn't be gone. As in, whoever hired the man would probably send someone else. But if it was the same person, it would also help to simplify things. But, she shook her head, that didn't fit. Not according to news report. "The guy that came after me," Erin said. "He was *big*. But the person they showed on the screen image was small."

The new report showed a fuzzy still taken from a security camera, and only of the suspect's back. Dark jacket, medium-length brown hair. It was pretty generic. But, Erin thought, as a chill ran up her back, it was an uncomfortably close description to *her*, too. She'd been there. Close to the time Senator Cleason was killed. Maybe even after.

It was for all of these reasons, Erin was jittery as she stood at Thomas Hale's front door, waiting. She had nothing but intuition. But it all felt a little too *just so*.

Erin reached up and knocked on the door again. This time harder, adding a few extra knocks. "What's taking him so long?" she said.

Ben shrugged, but didn't seem too bothered by it.

"How was he last time you saw him?"

"Suspended," Ben said, still looking at Hale's front door.

Right, Erin thought. *That.* In Colombia, she'd figured out pretty quickly that Hale fell more into the by-the-book camp than he did the renegade-for-the-law one. So she was surprised at how much he'd done down there. He'd taken a big risk. But, when it was all over, from Hale's point of view — and, most notably, from the *Bureau's* point of view — Colombia didn't go so well. She added that to her jitters. They were running out of allies, and she very much hoped Tom was still one.

The door opened. Hale stood, looking at the two. He looked at them for a moment, like they were holding a pizza he hadn't ordered. Then, as if snapping out of it, he stood aside, motioning them in.

"Get in," he said. He stood back, and as they walked in, he was almost pulling them inside. He took a quick careful look outside before shutting the door. He set the deadbolt as they walked farther inside.

"I'm guessing, you haven't heard yet?" Hale said.

"About Senator Cleason?" Erin said.

"No," Hale said, looking at Erin. "About you."

Erin looked to Ben, who didn't seem to know what Hale was talking about. The three of them were now in Hale's living room. It looked like he'd been making his last stand for the better part of a week now. And…she thought, he was losing the war. He was wearing old blue jeans and a plain white tee. As he walked to his computer, she wondered how long he'd been wearing that exact outfit.

Hale stood at his laptop on the kitchen bar and started clicking around. Neither Erin nor Ben sat. And Hale didn't say anything while he worked. Erin felt a little awkward standing there, waiting, watching him.

"So," she said, breaking the silence. "What did you mean, when you asked if I'd heard about *me*?"

He turned around, showing them his laptop. "FBI sent out an agency-wide email. They send these all the time. But this one, obviously caught my eye."

Erin looked at the screen and her pulse stopped.

She saw more security-camera stills, from the Dirksen building last night. But they weren't blurry, like the news reports were. They were sharp. And — she was having trouble breathing now — they were *her*. There was no doubt.

Hale clicked a button, showing more images.

Her face. They had her face on camera. "But what does…," she started. She looked at Hale and then Ben.

Ben walked away, rubbing his hands on his head.

"Tom…," Erin said, shaking her head.

Hale looked at her squarely.

"They think it was you who killed Senator Cleason."

27

WANTED

"THEY DIDN'T RELEASE THESE IMAGES TO THE PUBLIC," Hale explained. "Because they don't need the public's help finding you. The image they did release to the media was vague, on purpose. They do that sometimes, when they don't want to spook a suspect — but when they also need to show the public that they're doing something."

Erin let herself fall back onto Hale's couch, staring at nothing. Ben had been standing off to the side, quiet as he listened to Hale. He walked up to Hale. "So what do we do?" he said.

Hale opened his mouth to answer, but Erin started talking.

"I'll just…," she said, looking up at the other two. "Turn myself in."

Ben started slowly shaking his head. "No," he said. "That's not—"

"Listen," she said. "I'll cooperate. I'll give them whatever access they need. And they'll see it's not me. It couldn't be. Besides, I was there. Maybe I saw something that could help their investigation. It makes sense for me to—."

"Erin—" Ben said, cutting her off.

"What other play do we have?" she said. "If I run, I'm going to look guilty. You heard Tom, they haven't even released my name yet. Only a guilty person runs."

Hale was quiet.

Ben turned to him. "Hale," he said. "This is crazy. She can't…"

"He's right," Hale said, looking down at his carpet. He looked up at the two of them. "If this was a normal investigation… maybe. But this is a *United States* Senator we're talking about." He covered his mouth, as he seemed to realize something else. "And…," he swore under his breath as he turned around, starting to pace around his small living room. He turned back to the two of them. "They'll be tracking you," he said.

Erin looked from Hale to Ben.

"As in…," she said, pointing to the floor. "They know I'm here, right now?"

"Maybe," Hale said. "I don't know. But they will." He swore again.

Erin felt bad about that. She'd inadvertently dragged Hale into a federal murder investigation. He was suspended from the Bureau right now. But after this, he'd be lucky if he stayed out of prison. He seemed to be realizing this same thing. He was quiet. And so was Erin.

"Okay," Ben said, breaking the silence. "Let's think. A Senator has been murdered. The FBI already has their suspect. And they're not interested in the truth if it's too inconvenient. They're looking for someone they can reasonably convict." He was ticking these off on his fingers now. "And, it's safe to say, they're listening in and following you."

Erin was listening to him.

Hale was off on his own, trying to keep himself together.

"That means," Ben said. "We've only got one option."

"I need to run," Erin said quietly. She was half hoping someone would tell her another option. She was already feeling alone at the prospect of it.

"We," Ben said.

"What?"

"*We* need to run," he said. "There's no way any of us *aren't* going to look like accomplices. Plus," he added, "you think I'd miss this?" He said it with a smile. It was the last emotion she thought she'd ever feel again. But seeing him smile, even if he was putting on, made her feel a little bit better. Like, maybe, she wasn't all alone in this.

"Then we need to go," she said, standing up, finding a new resolve. She grabbed her jacket and began pulling it on.

Hale looked up, his world coming back into theirs. "Go?" he said. "Where are you going to go?"

Erin opened her mouth to answer. But then closed it again. *He was right.* She stopped putting her jacket on. If they were already looking for her — and they hadn't made that public yet — then one of the first places they'd go would be to her house.

"Gavin…," she said. "He's still at my house. They'll think he's an accomplice and take him in. We have to warn him."

"How?" Ben said. "They'll be listening in. They'll be on us as soon as we try."

Hale spoke again. "They probably already are," he said. "I'm suspended for my involvement in Colombia. Which you" — he motioned to Erin — "were at the center of. It won't be long before they figure it out."

Erin pulled out her cell phone, to call Gavin.

"No," Hale said, reaching out to stop her from dialing.

"Why? You said they'll already—"

Hale was looking around, his eyes darting at different places on the floor. She could tell he was working through something. "No," he repeated. "They *will* check here, yes.

But they'll follow protocol first. If we alert them, they'll be on us faster. But right now, if we don't, we've still got a head start."

"A headstart for *what* exactly?" Erin asked, still holding her cell phone. But…she already knew the answer. She was hoping Hale would have something, some FBI resource or knowledge that they didn't know about. But he didn't.

"To run," he said simply.

28

GAVIN

Gavin swore, letting the Venetian blinds snap back into place. He saw a dark van down the street. The sidewalks were strangely vacant. They were probably herding people off of the street, out of sight. He swore again.

After Erin and Ben left, Gavin started digging. They needed to find out who was behind Cleason's murder. At the very least, so that they knew who they were dealing with. But, more practically, so that they could figure out what their next move was. Ben hadn't been clear on exactly *what* Paul had in mind for Gavin to do. But at this point, it didn't matter. He was in his element. And whether this was part of the plan or not, he knew what needed to be done.

By normal standards, Gavin was a hacker. Personally, it was a label he hated. It gave the impression he was doing something illegal. But that wasn't true. The area most 'hackers' played in wasn't clearly regulated. It was technical. Hacking wasn't intrinsically about doing illicit things. It was about exploring. About founding the boundaries and discovering unclaimed treasures. He'd been looking around for about an hour or so, but he hadn't found anything helpful yet. That hadn't deterred him. This could easily be a long process.

The government, for their part, had its fair share of flaws on the digital front. But, *unlike* the movies, hacking into government systems wasn't easy. Not — that is — if you wanted to do it safely. And avoid a holy armageddon of federal agents breaking down your front door. Which Gavin definitely did *not* want. And so Gavin was being careful, covering his tracks, continuing to search.

Considering recent events — the murder of Senator Cleason — Gavin was pulling out all the stops and taking every precaution he could think of. He'd pulled up a digital police scanner feed someone had posted on a forum. It was old school. But that's the thing about 'hacking.' Most of it wasn't digital hacking — it was *human* hacking. And… the old school stuff was often the easiest to access.

He set the range to a five-mile radius from Erin's address. It had mostly been normal police chatter. And he'd been mostly tuning it out. But then, a few minutes ago, something caught his attention.

It was Erin's street name.

He turned it up, tightened the parameters a bit, and listened in. It was fairly cryptic, the police operators used so much code and shorthand it almost sounded like another language. But he could tell something was about to happen. That's when he went to the front window.

No, correction, he now knew something had *already started* happening.

29

AN IDEA

Erin felt like she was being dragged along. She wished there was another way. A way that didn't involve her becoming a fugitive and, not to mention, leaving Gavin behind. She knew he was going to be picked up. Booked as an accomplice.

"Come on," Ben said. "He's smart, Gavin. He'll be fine."

They were standing next to Hale's white Ford Explorer, in the parking garage, connected to his apartment. Hale was still inside, getting a few things.

"If we run," she said. "We lose everything. Including all of Paul's research. And the proof of what Eli Bren has done. There has to be another way. It's too great a risk."

"There's not," Ben said. "And" — he looked at her — "we don't lose *everything*." He smiled. And she smiled back, weakly. She knew what he meant. And she knew it was true. Even though it didn't feel like it right now. She nodded and got into the back seat. Hale's Explorer had tinted windows. The idea was for her to stay out of sight, so Hale and Ben would ride upfront. According to Hale, neither of them would be a top target (yet). And so they still had a little bit of time to get out of the city. Ben shut her door and walked around and got into the front passenger seat.

Hale walked up with a duffel bag. He opened the back of the SUV and tossed it in.

"We can stop and buy clothes and stuff for you guys when we're out of the city," he said, from the back. He shut the door and walked around to the driver's seat. He got in and shut his door, starting the engine.

"So, where is this place?" Ben said.

Hale looked around and reversed out of his parking spot. "It's about three hours out of the city," he said. "Through Virginia and into West Virginia."

"This place," Ben said. "It's yours?"

"Sort of," Hale said, navigating the tight parking garage. "It belongs to my family."

The Explorer pulled out of the parking garage and drove into midday Washington D.C. traffic.

"Have you ever heard of Lost River, West Virginia?" Hale asked.

"No," Ben said.

"It's the nearest city. Pretty remote. Bad cell phone service, one grocery store. That sort of thing."

"That's where your family's farm is?" Ben asked.

"No," Hale said. "The farm is another fifteen or twenty minutes beyond that. It's isolated," he said, looking into his rearview mirror. Erin saw him glance at her. "It'll give us a good place to regroup."

Erin watched the cars out of her window as Hale continued to drive. All of them, so normal. Going about life, work, and school. The Explorer passed a woman, about Erin's age, wearing sunglasses and driving a minivan. Erin guessed she had a kid or two in the back. For a moment, she was lost in their world. Or what she imagined it to be. Where the woman was going, how old her kids were, what kind of problems she'd have to deal with today. And for now, she sighed, daydreaming about someone else was about as close to normal as Erin could get.

30

GONE

GAVIN RAN THROUGH ERIN'S DOWNSTAIRS, ALMOST knocking an end table over as he did. He'd brought a bag with him when he'd come and he was now throwing everything he could think of into it. Erin's laptop was on her coffee table. He reached for it, and then paused. They'd probably be tracking it. If not yet, soon. He left it. He slid his own computer into his bag. Along with a handful of cables.

He ran back to the front and carefully looked out of the blinds. The van was still there. He looked at it hard for a moment. He thought he could see movement inside. But the windows were dark. He ran back to the living room and picked up his bag, trying to remember the neighborhood layout. It was dark when he arrived. But he was pretty sure it wasn't one of those closed neighborhoods, with only one way in and out.

He opened the back door. A burst of cold air hit him. He'd forgotten his jacket. He turned around and grabbed it. And then, looking around as best he could, he slipped out Erin's backdoor. Her backyard was small, surrounded by a wooden fence. Behind it, was her neighbor's backyard. Gavin put his hands on top of the wooden fence, and jumped up, snatching a look at what was on the other side. In the half-second he was in the air, he saw the neighbor's backyard: a few kids toys and no people.

Good.

But… there was no way he was getting over that fence. He looked around and behind him for other options. Leaving through the front was a sure way to get caught. Erin's backyard was pretty empty, except for a couple metal chairs on her back patio. He dropped his bag in the grass and ran over to grab one. They were surprisingly heavy. Like actual cast iron. He dragged it to the other side of her yard and set it up against the fence. It was cold outside, but he could feel he was already beginning to sweat.

He picked up his bag and stepped into the chair. He could see over the fence now. Still clear. He tossed his bag over and then, threw a leg up.

Except, his leg didn't catch on and fell back down stupidly.

He took a deep breath and tried again, this time with a bit of a jump behind it. And…it worked! Sort of… His shoe was hooked (and stayed) on the top of the fence — which was good. But his other leg was still very much down below on the chair, holding the rest of him. He was doing a kind of bad split. One leg down, doing a little hop on the heavy chair below him, while his other leg stayed put on top of the fence.

He now realized, the easy part had been getting his first leg up. The hard part would be getting the rest of him up and over. He put his hands on the edge, and tried jumping. No dice. He was still stuck, like an idiot. He glanced around, hoping none of the five houses whose backyards now had a full and direct line of sight to him, didn't catch a glimpse of this. It would be hard to explain under *good* circumstances.

He took another breath, bouncing on his foot below, already feeling his muscles getting tired. He tried again. But, this time, miraculously, it worked. He hefted the rest of his weight up, rolling right on top of the thin old wooden fence — balancing and swearing all at the same time.

And then, before he'd realized what was happening, he rolled off the other side, leaving behind only his dignity. Fortunately, the bag he'd packed his laptop in broke his fall.

Erin's neighbor's grass was bitter in his mouth. He tried spitting it out, but his mouth was dry. He stood up, feeling about fourteen different shots of pain, all, conveniently, from different parts of his body. He reached down, collected his breath and his bag, and turned to leave.

Except…he wasn't alone.

In his haste, he was beginning to realize, he hadn't done quite a thorough enough job in scouting out his escape route. On a small, primary-colored trike, sat a small face with large eyes, mouth open, staring at him. The kid was like a little statue.

"Hey buddy," Gavin said, putting on his best 'kid' voice.

The last time he was around a kid he'd been one. He didn't know what to say. He caught himself looking for a stick to pick up and throw in the opposite direction. Like fetch or something. No…that's for dogs.

Gavin raised his hand in a little wave.

The kid didn't move. Just sat on his trike, still holding the handles, feet still on the pedals, frozen. He stared unblinkingly at Gavin.

Gavin took a step forward, and the kid's mouth quivered. And then, his eyes began to shift from no-compute to an unspeakable form of terror. Gavin was watching it, like it was happening in slow motion. The kid was filling his lungs. Like a pitcher, winding up for the big strikeout. Any minute now…

"No, no, no," Gavin started, talking as softly as he could, still holding out his hand. But this only seemed to exacerbate the situation. And the banshee scream that followed was every bit what the kid's face had promised it would be.

Gavin swore, feeling bad about that — in front of the kid — but then again, he probably couldn't hear anything over his own wailing. Gavin dropped all pretense and ran as fast as he could, across the kid's yard, heading for their front gate. As he did, he saw the kid's backdoor open. Probably the Mom coming out to see which of the neighbors was assaulting Junior. Gavin reached the wooden gate, and started fiddled with, trying to get it open.

"Hey," he heard behind him. *Nope*, not the mom. Definitely the dad.

"So— so sorry," Gavin called out over his shoulder, without turning around, still trying to get the ridiculously stubborn gate latch open.

"Stop," the man yelled.

Got it. Gate open.

Gavin ran full out, as hard as he could. His bag was slinging wildly on his back behind him. It wasn't a pretty sight. But then again, neither was going to a federal penitentiary. He kept running until he got to the busy street and then turned, almost immediately collapsing into a sweaty mess of jacket, bag, and general disheveledness. As he sat, heaving for breath, the cold wind blew over his face. An older man, walking by, stopped and leaned down. "You okay, son?" Gavin raised a hand and nodded in response, it was the best he could do, while his lungs continued to burn for oxygen. The man walked away with what Gavin interpreted as a disapproving look. But, considering all the rest…he could live with that.

31

THE FARM

ERIN OPENED HER EYES. MUST HAVE DOZED OFF. AFTER a thankfully boring three hour drive — most of which was winding through the backroad highways of Maryland and West Virginia — the Explorer pulled off onto a dusty gravel road.

Hale was still driving, but slower now. Erin looked out the window at the countryside. Looking at it, she felt like it was a thousand miles from D.C. That alone brought some comfort. The sun was beginning to set. She looked down at her watch. She might have dozed for longer than she'd thought.

The Explorer came to a stop in the middle of nowhere. Erin sat up, adjusted her seat belt, and looked through the front windshield.

"I got it," Ben said, hopping out.

She saw him walk around the front of the Explorer, unhook a metal gate and drag it out of the way. It didn't have hinges. It was just chained on one side, hooked on the other.

"It's for the cows," Hale said to Erin.

"So your mom really does live on a farm," she said. "I thought that was figurative," she added.

Outside, Ben stood aside and Hale drove the Explorer a few feet forward, stopping it again when he was just inside the fenced area. Behind them, Ben was shutting the gate.

Erin looked out of her window. "It's huge," she said.

"Not as big as the one we grew up on," Hale said. "The one I grew up on, back in Nebraska, that was a real farm. Mom only moved out here after dad died. It's close to D.C., which means close to me. And it's got a few cows and horses to keep her busy."

Ben got back in and Hale started driving. The gravel crunched under the Explorer's tires as the vehicle bumped and swayed over the dirt road. It was another moment of driving before Erin saw a house. Then, not far behind that, she saw a barn and what looked like stables.

Standing on the drive, waiting for them was a woman, dressed in old jeans and a plaid shirt. Despite the cold, she had her sleeves rolled up. Her hair was long, streaked with gray, and pulled back.

"That's mom," Hale said, slowing to a stop and turning off the engine.

The three of them got out and Hale's mom walked up to him and gave him a hug. He introduced her to Erin and Ben.

"It's nice to meet you, Ms. Hale," Erin said, offering her hand to shake.

"Just Celia," she said, ignoring her hand and pulling Erin into a hug. Her slender frame was stronger than Erin expected. And she was warm. Celia gave Ben a hug, too. And then, turning to everyone, she said, "Let's go inside. It's getting cold." As she walked inside, the other three followed. "I hope you're hungry," she said over her shoulder.

Erin was hungry. Outside of D.C., they stopped for her and Ben to buy a change of clothes. The other two ate lunch when they were stopped. But Erin wasn't in the mood. However, she was now regretting that decision. Celia mother-henned them inside and sat them at her small wooden table. It had three places already set. Erin was surprised — Celia wasn't kidding, she really did have food waiting for them. She walked to the stove and took a pot off the burner. Ben offering to help. But Celia wasn't having any of it. Hale seemed to be taking it all in stride.

"In that case," Ben said. "Can I use your restroom?"

"Down that way," she said, pointing to a hall without looking. "Second on the left."

As Ben left, Erin leaned over to Hale. "How did she know we were…?"

"I called her from a payphone," Hale said. "When we filled up for gas."

Erin didn't remember that. And her face must have said the same.

"You were asleep," he said.

She did remember dozing, but she must have been out longer than she realized.

"How long was I out?"

"A while," Hale said.

Ben walked back in and sat down. Celia put plates in front of them. And she sat down with a plate for herself, too. Before they began eating, she had them all go around and say something they were each thankful for. Erin had never had this kind of family experience, but it was oddly comforting. Ben seemed to immediately take to it.

Of all the things that had taken a sharp dive sideways recently, this wasn't one of them. Being here, feeling the solace of Hale's mother's farm. A temporary relief from the quick and dangerous storm outside.

The three of them were looking at Erin now. It was her time to say something. She didn't know what she was thankful for. Or, rather, she wasn't accustomed to thinking about it in such a specific way. She looked at the other three.

"This," she said finally. "Being here."

Celia bowed her head and said a short prayer. She spoke, presumably to God, and told him what everyone was thankful for. And then, she added something Erin found curious. "Thank you for your goodness to us," she said, still talking to God.

Erin was certainly thankful for what Celia had done. Taking them in. And, as Celia prayed, there were a hundred other things that popped into her head. Things she was thankful for. Other people. People who'd taken chances on her. Who'd risked their *lives* for her.

She wasn't sure how much of that had to do with God, per se. But, as she sat there, listening to Celia pray, she realized with an overwhelming sense, that she had a lot to be thankful for. And, despite everything that was going on, and all the uncertainties of it, life *was* good.

32

"WIFI'S EXTRA"

"I need a credit card," the woman behind the counter said.

"Your sign says you take cash," Gavin said, pointing to the sign eighteen inches away, on the counter between them.

The woman smacked her gum and cut her eyes to look at the sign, like she was genuinely annoyed to see it really sitting there. She took a moment to get a few more chews in. Apparently reading it over, to make sure there was no hidden clause where 'cash or credit accepted' meant something other than cash or credit accepted. She looked back at Gavin.

"Fine," she said. "But you'll have to pay a deposit."

"Fine," Gavin said.

"And you don't get it back if you trash the place."

Gavin looked around. Based on the lobby — which, he assumed was probably in better shape than the rooms — he thought he'd have to work pretty hard to 'trash the place.'

"Okay," Gavin said again.

"It's two nights, the deposit," she said, still watching him. "And wifi's extra," she added.

"Whatever," Gavin said, shifting his bag's weight on his

back and pulling out his wallet. He put the cash down on the counter, and the woman took it.

Gavin had always preferred to be as under-the-radar as he could. And even though he lived on the bleeding edge of the digital world, his financial life still resided comfortably in the previous century's cash-based economy.

And it was a strange thing to have in common with someone as different from him as Millicent Beaumont. Coincidentally, they both shared a strong distrust of the government. For Gavin, it was about not wanting to be spied on or profiled. For Millicent Beaumont, she didn't like someone else tapping into her small fortune. She's called paying taxes "the rape" of "honest hardworking people." Gavin found this a little bit ironic, since on multiple other occasions she'd told him that she hadn't actually earned any of her money, but was carrying on, stewarding the estate her late father built.

Due to Gavin's employment situation — or lack thereof — after returning from Ghana, he'd been living for free with his brother, while he saved un-taxed cash from Millicent Beaumont. He'd planned to put it into a deposit on an apartment or something. Not rent a room at a seedy hotel.

The woman dropped a key on the counter, eying him.

"And it's just you?" she said.

"Yeah," Gavin said.

"It's around the side," she said, referring to the room. He shifted his weight, adjusting his bag. He looked at her. Expecting to have to sign something. Or, at least, to give her his name.

"That all?" he said.

She looked at him, taking her face to a genuinely new level of annoyance. She rested her hand on her counter, as if he might be the kind of trouble she'd have to get in line at some point.

"This is not *that* kind of motel," she said.

He then realized, given the look on her face, the location of this dump, and its low price, that this was *exactly* that kind of motel. Probably quite a few clandestine, one-hour afternoon meetings had happened here. And she must have thought that he was looking for some, uh, *assistance* in that area.

"Never mind," he said, grabbing the key from the counter. He turned around and walked back outside. He could hear the buzz of the fluorescent "vacant" sign as he walked through the glass front door. He let the door slam behind him and went to find his room.

33

HER

Erin woke up with the sun streaming into her window. Celia's ranch-style house was a lot bigger on the inside than it looked on the outside. She had enough room to give them each their own place to sleep. Erin had slept in a proper guest room, with a bed and its own bathroom. Ben was sleeping in another room. And Hale had been in a sleeping bag in a room that wasn't a bedroom.

Erin pulled on some clothes — yesterday's jeans and a new, unwashed sweatshirt they'd picked up on the way out of D.C. She took a minute to collect herself. She was feeling surprisingly good. Full of energy. And optimism. She opened her door and walked down the short hall. Celia's house matched the farm it was on. It had a homey rustic feel to it. But at the same time, it was all clean and manicured. The exposed wood beams added another layer of warmth to the place.

In the kitchen, Ben and Hale were already sitting at the table. It looked like they had already eaten. Celia was standing near the coffee pot. And by her outfit, Erin figured she'd already been outside working.

"How did you sleep?" Celia asked as Erin walked in.

"Good," she said. "Really good, actually."

Celia was pouring herself a cup of coffee. "Here," she said, using the coffee pot to motion for Erin to grab a mug. They were hanging nearby on a decorative wooden rack. Erin grabbed one and Celia filled it with coffee.

"Thanks," she said. Erin walked over to the table where Ben and Hale were sitting and joined them. Their breakfast plates were off to the side.

Celia, steaming coffee in hand, turned to walk back to the door. "I know you guys have a lot of work to do," she said. "I'm going to be outside. I've got a bit more to do here. And, Erin, honey, breakfast is there," she said, motioning to the counter with her coffee mug. "Help yourself."

Erin looked to the counter and saw biscuits and bacon, among other things that Celia had apparently prepared. Celia left and Erin looked over at Hale.

"Has she always been like this?"

He smiled. "Yeah," he said. "Mother hen."

Erin sipped on her coffee and looked over at Ben and then back to Hale. The two of them were quiet. Almost, Erin felt, too quiet.

"What?" she said.

Hale opened his mouth to speak. And then, shut it again.

"We were...," Ben started. "Eh — figuring out re-entry."

"Re-entry?" Erin said.

"D.C.," Hale said. "We're safe here. For now. Internet is non-existent here, which means, while tracking is not impossible, it's definitely slower. But there's a limit to how long we can push that."

"And," Ben added, "we're going to have to figure this out. And soon. Tom and I" — he nodded across the table — "were talking, before you woke up. It's clear that Eli Bren has been ahead of us every step of the way."

The optimism that Erin had woken up with was starting, slowly, to dwindle. "Yeah," she said with a nod. "I've certainly noticed that."

"Right," Hale said. "So here's what we *do* know. Bren knew Paul was building a case against him. And a good one, apparently, because he sent someone to recover it. He also knew you had accessed it. That," he continued, "was evident because he sent someone after you in D.C. He must have assumed you knew more than you should."

"But," Erin said. "We don't actually know the man who came after me was *from* Bren."

"That's true," Ben said. "But it's a pretty safe bet. Think about the timing. Just after you sent some of the evidence you'd found to Senator Cleason, he was no longer available to meet. Which would have been suspicious if he hadn't turned up dead the next morning.

"And," Hale added. "That same night, around the time Cleason was killed, someone came after you."

Erin looked back down into her coffee and let out a low breath. "Yeah," she said.

Hale was now holding up fingers as he ticked off his and Ben's points. "And that brings us to the last big thing," he said. "You're being framed. And it's a good enough frame that the F.B.I. is convinced."

Erin took a sip of her coffee and set it back down on the wooden table. She stood up and walked to the counter, picking up a biscuit but not looking at it. She took a bite and walked back to where Ben and Hale were sitting. "So what *doesn't* Eli Bren know?" she asked, more to herself than anyone in particular. She took another bite of her biscuit and pulled Ben's plate over to catch her crumbs.

"Jonah Lennox," Hale said. "Well, possibly..."

Erin thought about that. Jonah had found out about Morocco from Val. Which meant he was still pretty close to her. And whatever was happening in D.C., with Senator Cleason's death and her being framed, Erin bet it had to do with Val. She knew from talking to Paul about Val that she'd been an assassin for her entire adult life.

And as she was thinking about this, a new theory began to bud in her mind. Val had a similar frame and build as Erin. While Erin was at Senator Cleason's office — an undeniable fact — it could have been possible for Val, dressed like Erin, to have also been there. Seeing the two from the back, with the right clothes and hairstyle, Val could appear to be her.

And then, as recently as the night before last, Jonah knew the man was coming after her. Hale might be right. He very well could still be connected to Eli.

"I think that could work," she said finally. "Using Jonah as an entry point."

"Yeah…," Ben said. "But do you think it *would* work? I mean, do you really think we can trust him?"

Erin didn't have to think about that. She wasn't ready to justify her position on the matter. But she knew, somewhere deep down, that…*yes*. They, or she, could trust Jonah Lennox.

She nodded to both of them. And then picked up the next step in the logic. "I think, though," she said. "The bigger problem is what we're going to do now that all of Paul's research is gone. If the F.B.I. is looking for me, then they've certainly been to my home by now. Meaning, everything we had on Eli is now with the F.B.I."

"I thought about that, too," Hale said. "Anything that doesn't give them an immediate clue to your whereabouts right now will go straight to an evidence locker."

The three of them were silent. Erin took another sip of her coffee, but it was cold now. She got up to get more. They tossed around a few more ideas. Each of them as improbable or outlandish as the last.

Eli Bren, it seemed, was winning.

But… Erin couldn't help but thinking — there was one more angle they hadn't talked about.

Her.

From Paul's notes, she knew the history between Bren and her mother. That they'd had an affair. And that Bren was her biological father. But according to Paul's notes, and his notes were quite detailed in some areas, there wasn't any indication that Gillian, her mother, had told Bren about Erin. No child support. They'd never lived together. And the affair itself was pretty short-lived.

A fresh idea was finding its way around her mind.

But there was one thing that was standing in the way. Bren had tried to kill her. Possibly even twice now. Once in D.C., two days ago. And the other time in Morocco, the week before. Though, there was a nagging hope, still, somehow alive in all of this. He *hadn't* killed her in Bogotá, when he clearly had the chance. Through Val, he had killed Paul. And Rafael, off to the side, shot and bleeding, already looked dead. She was that last loose end that day.

But he didn't do it…

When they were last face to face, why hadn't he done it?

Her theory was thin, and she knew it. Almost too thin to say out loud. And certainly too thin to actually turn into a plan they could pull off.

But…

"I think," she said, to the other two. "I think there might be another option."

34

GOT YOU

GAVIN WAS SITTING IN A COFFEE SHOP, EARBUDS IN, buried in his laptop. He slept well last night. Considering the motel room he stayed in looked like it was used for everything but sleeping, and the neon vacant sign outside his window buzzed like a thousand permanent hornets, and, of course, there was that little thing about almost being caught by the F.B.I. or whoever was casing Erin's house.

But Gavin had a gift. He could turn all that off. As soon as he closed his eyes, he was out. It was something that helped him adapt so well to life overseas.

The next morning, he took a quick shower, grabbed his bag, and called a ride to take him, indiscriminately, to whatever the nearest coffee shop was. Starbucks, It turned out to be. Of course. That had been around six this morning. It was now almost lunchtime, and — except for a few bathroom breaks and coffee refills — he hadn't moved from his seat.

He'd been working on something very specific. Or, rather, two somethings.

Before everything happened yesterday, Gavin had a theory he hadn't shared with the rest. Based on what Erin had told him, he was beginning to believe that someone was tracking Erin's phone. It would have been how they found her in Morocco, again in D.C., and then how they knew exactly when she was at the Senator's office. He didn't have any actual proof of that yet. But it all fit.

And so yesterday morning, while she and Ben were talking, he borrowed her phone and cloned it. Not the whole thing, like her messages. Just its signature: its MAC address and a few other digital 'thumbprints.' The process itself wasn't hard. He'd developed something similar when he was in Ghana, but he'd never had a chance to use it. In rural settings, everyone — no matter how poor their living conditions are — had a prepaid mobile phone of some sort. And so the program Gavin developed helped them track disease outbreaks, as well as other movements, by simply having them text a message to a number, swap their SIM card for a new one, or any of a few other ways that would allow Gavin to peel off the metadata he needed to register them.

It only took a few seconds, in Erin's living room yesterday, for Gavin to grab her phone's signature. And because then he still had quite a few options, he didn't bother mentioning to them what he'd done. The plan was, he'd use her phone's info he grabbed to run back up the channels and see where the tracking was happening — and, most importantly, *who* was doing it.

But grabbing her phone's signature was the easy part. Everything after that was of the manual old-school detective-work fashion. One of those old-fashioned tricks was tapping a friend with access to the national register of cellphone towers. Cellphone towers are not owned by a single wireless provider. Instead, carriers rent access. And how much they rent — and where — determines the bulk of their service quality and coverage. His friend gave him access back when he was doing pro bono work for an NGO. Gavin was putting together the tech side of a fundraising proposal. It wasn't strictly legal, his friend giving him access. But, basically, the rule was: look and don't touch. As long as Gavin's network traffic stayed small and didn't do anything that would show up on anyone's radar, then it was a no-harm, no-foul situation.

That was several years ago now. Earlier this morning, Gavin gave the credentials a try again. And not only had the passwords *not* changed in the last few years, but they apparently didn't have any alarms or ways of ferreting out if someone like him was doing something like what he was now doing. Gavin was pretty sure he was way over the 'under the radar' limit. But at this point, he didn't care.

And, so far, he'd learned a lot.

The cell tower registry didn't do any of the heavy processing. It was just for gathering raw data. But once Gavin had that data, he ran it through a few other modeling programs — software mostly designed for tracking diseases and their spread — and he was able to learn two important things.

First, someone *was* shadowing Erin's phone. Or he was pretty sure of it. Because he had access to the entire East Coast's cell phone towers, he could compare her current activity to her previous activity. And while she hadn't been back for very long (meaning he didn't really have a big enough dataset to be statistically significant) it did give him a pretty good idea of what was going on.

He sent a few pieces of data over to another friend. Well, not a friend per se, but someone who owed him a few big favors. He only knew him by his handle online. *Aegeates.* The story was, Aegeates picked the name of an obscure ancient Roman governor: big, but at the same time, obscure. A lot of people lived online like this. And Aegeates was big in a few online RPG games. And so he'd made a name for himself there. He did jobs like this, 'real-world' things, not for money, but for bragging rights.

Gavin texted Aegeates through an encrypted app. Giving him a screenshot and a few pieces of data, he asked him if he could figure out who was tracking her. No response. Gavin put his phone back down on the coffee shop table, next to his empty paper coffee cups, and waited.

The second big thing he learned this morning was the results from the program he'd been running. The cell phone registry's numbers he'd been crunching. He watched the digital timer on his screen, counting down until it was done processing. *Three, two, and...*

"Got you," he said under his breath.

A phone that's been turned off still does a little check-in routine with its nearest cell phone tower. This is part security feature and part convenience. Even in off-mode, most of our devices still have a small part of them that's still on. You can see evidence of this when you turn your phone on after its been off for a while, and you immediately have alerts waiting for you. It doesn't pull in all the data associated with those alerts. But it does do a basic hand-shake, your device tells home base: here I am. Also, another indication is that your settings are all still where you left them when you power back up. Even in off mode, part of the phone is still on and working.

This is what Gavin used to find Erin's phone. Yesterday, once he figured out a government agency was actively looking for Erin — and knowing also that she went to see an F.B.I. friend — he was pretty sure she would have figured it out and not come back home. And, if she'd thought about it, she would probably have turned her phone off in the process. For security.

Which, to her credit, *did* help some.

A turned-off phone only talks to home base once every

now and then. It relays two things. One, the general geographic area the phone is in — in this case, a radius of about five miles. And two, how long the phone had been in that spot. As in, is it still moving, or is it sitting still? Erin's phone, Gavin saw, was sitting still.

He copied her GPS coordinates into Google Maps. It pulled up a few roads, spread out, and a large empty area. No Street View was available, probably too rural, he figured. From what he could tell, it looked like she was in a big field or something. He backed down the road on the map until Google's Street View was available. He saw a small town. He guessed she was visiting an old friend or something.

Gavin's phone on the table buzzed. He picked it up, knocking over one of his empty paper coffee cups in the process. It was Aegeates, with a single letter response.

y

How long, Gavin typed back.

Aegeates' response was immediate.

2h

Gavin saved all of his work and then put an extra copy on a flash drive, which he slipped into his pocket. He closed the lid of his laptop, dropped it in his bag, and, leaving his eight paper coffee cups on the table where he was sitting all morning, walked outside. He opened his ridesharing app and called for a car. The sun was irritatingly bright. The cold wind whipped around and through him.

He stood leaning against the outside of the Starbucks. He looked down at his phone again, seeing the little map with his car icon. The car was on the way now. Four minutes. He was beginning to nurse a headache. Maybe it was the sun. He'd done good work this morning, including figuring out how someone was following Erin. In a few more hours, and with a little luck, Aegeates would have the name of who was doing it.

35

CHRISTMAS

"No way," Ben said.

Erin looked at Hale, who was looking equally skeptical.

"What other play do we have here?" Erin said.

Ben put out his hands, like he was trying to talk her off a ledge. "That's what we're going to figure out," he said.

"Think about it," Erin said. "He's my *dad*. And there's a good chance he doesn't know that. If I can just meet with him, face to face—"

"Erin—" Hale said.

"It'd be in a public place," she said. "Safe."

Ben folded his arms and was looking down at the table, slowly shaking his head.

"There's just no way," Hale said. "The guy's a psychopath."

"But he didn't do anything in Colombia, when he had the chance," Erin said.

"Didn't *do* anything?" Ben said, looking up.

"To me, I mean," Erin said.

"Maybe," Ben said, looking back down at the table again,

thinking. "Or maybe he just wanted to follow you to Paul's storehouse."

"I don't think so," she said. "How would he have known about it, that early? *We* didn't."

"I don't know," Ben said. "But this…isn't the way."

Hale shifted his weight in his seat. "Look. Erin," he said. "I'm with you, we need to do something. But Ben's right. The risk is too great, and the reward is too…thin. Think about it, we'd have to pull that off *while* you're an active — no, primary — F.B.I. suspect in the murder of a U.S. Senator."

The table was quiet. Hale was still looking at Erin. But she wasn't making eye contact with either of them. She stood up and walked to the door. She grabbed her jacket off the door hanger and put it on. She put her hand out, touching the wall, to stabilize herself and slid on her tennis shoes. She reached down, tied them, and then walked back to the counter and grabbed a biscuit. She still hadn't looked over at the other two, but she could feel them watching her. She turned back around, to go outside.

"Where are you going?" Ben said.

She didn't answer. She needed to get away. To think. She pulled the door open. The wind hit her face. It was cold outside. Colder than she remembered. And then, quite randomly, a thought hit her. It was December. *Late* December. And she noticed, for the first time since arriving, a modest green garland set around the outside of Celia's door frame. For Christmas. Christmas was coming.

She turned back to the two of them, both still watching her.

"What's today?" she asked.

"Today?" Hale said.

"It's, uh, Tuesday…," Ben said.

"No," Erin said. "The date."

Hale looked down at his watch. "It's…," he made a face, as if it surprised him, too. "It's the twenty-fourth." He said, looking up at her. "It's Christmas Eve."

She turned around and walked outside, shutting the door behind her.

36

HORSES

The day rolled on. Celia was in and out. Erin was surprised at how much it took to run a farm. Even a "small one," as Hale put it. Though, Erin didn't have much basis for what small or large was in this context.

The three of them, Erin, Ben, and Hale continued to work through a few plans. Most of their scenarios centered on getting Paul's files back from the F.B.I. and continuing the investigation, or making a case for Erin's innocence. But none of them were very promising. And, as Hale reminded her more than a few times, the chance of her spending a few months in jail — even if it were just while things were being sorted out — was quite high. And those were the *happy* scenarios.

As the day moved on, Erin was also beginning to feel lonely. She wanted to reach out to Conall McGillis, her editor and longtime friend. But she knew, doing that would only put him in danger. She missed Paul, too. Throughout the years, she's never been close-close to him. But he was always there. Always available. And then, after seeing all the details he'd collected over the years, she understood that he was closer than she'd known.

She pushed those thoughts away, fearing they'd take her somewhere dangerous if she gave them too much space. She pushed herself to focusing instead on right now. A plan. Their time was ticking away. Soon they'd have to do something. Staying here much longer wasn't an option. Eventually, the F.B.I. would find her, bring Celia in as an accomplice, and then, whatever chance Erin had of proving her innocence would be seen through the tainted lens of being a fugitive. Nothing was looking good right now.

Erin was walking around the farm now. Thinking. The cold wind was blowing her hair. She pushed her hands into her jacket and turned to walk into the stables, where Celia kept the horses. It was mid afternoon now. Three of the horses were out in the field. But one was stabled. Erin walked up to him. Or her, she wasn't sure. Its massive head was hanging out over the half wall. Erin pulled a hand out of her jacket and reached out, to pet it. The horse pulled back. For all their size and bulk, horses were not bold creatures.

"Here," came a voice from behind her.

It was Celia. She was holding out a hand brush with long tan bristles. "Use this," she said. "Brush her this way." She modeled for Erin, how to brush the horse, and handed the brush to her to try. The horse was accustomed to the brush and leaned in, expecting it, all skittishness gone.

"They're a lot like people," Celia said. "They're scared of what they don't know, even if your intentions are pure. And," she added, "if you're not careful" — she reached over the half wall and rubbed the horse's side — "there's a lot of power here. And they can do real damage."

The two stood there for a moment, Erin continued to brush the horse, listening to the horse's breath.

Celia spoke again. "I'm sorry about your mother," she said.

"Thanks," Erin said, without looking at her. She'd heard this most of her life now. People find out her mother was a promising journalist, killed in action, leaving Erin as a little kid without parents. It seemed to touch people. And if she cared to talk about it, she would be tempted to use it more.

"And," Celia continued. "I overheard a little about your father. I don't know any of the details," she added shaking her head, as if she felt she might be overstepping. "But I do know you're in a pickle right now. A big one."

Erin didn't respond. She just continued to bush the horse as Celia talked. Celia had picked up another brush, and was bushing the horse's side as she talked.

"As a parent," Celia said. "It's… I don't know. It's hard to explain — to tell your kids what you already know. Kids," she shook her head, "they're vulnerable. But… at the same time, they're not. Kids — and really, all people — they've got much more inside them than most ever know. Honestly, it wasn't something I understood about myself until I became a parent."

Erin wasn't really sure why Celia was telling her these things. She didn't strike her as a talker. The two continued to bush the horse, Erin listening as Celia talked.

"Kids have more of their parents in them than they realize. And they've got more leverage over the world than they realize. It's just that," Celia said, letting out a sigh "and I know I'm overstepping here. But, whatever you're wrestling with, don't look at the consequence."

Celia put her bush down, and leaned on the half wall, looking at Erin. Erin didn't meet her eyes.

"Only God knows what the future holds. And unless I've missed something, he hasn't shared any of that with us. The only thing we can really do is what *we* can do. The things we know in our heart that *need* to be done. Anyway," she said, hanging up her brush, "I've found, when I'm facing a difficult decision, remembering that helps simplify things."

Erin realized she'd stopped brushing. The horse was pushing her large head up against the bush, her attempt to prompt Erin to continue. Erin gave her another stroke and handed the brush back to Celia, not meeting her eyes.

"Thanks," Erin said, looking up at her. "I appreciate it. Everything," she added. Erin turned, to walk out of the barn.

"Erin," Celia called out.

She stopped and turned, looking at her.

"You know I can't tell you what you should do. No one can. But I can tell you this," she said. "A parent — a real parent — doesn't stop loving their child, no matter what they do. But...," she hesitated. "Even real parents, sometimes, they need to learn that as well."

Erin looked at Celia for a long moment. A strong gust of wind whipped through the stables, flipping her hair in her eyes. Erin reached up, pulling her hair back.

"Celia," she said. "Can I use your phone? It's long distance."

She was talking about her land line. Celia didn't have a cell phone. Another feature of living on a remote farm and not having much of any out-side life. And Erin needed to make a call, before she lost her nerve to do it.

She smiled back. "Of course, honey. It's in the kitchen."

37

A CAR

ERIN WALKED THE LENGTH OF THE FARM. CELIA'S WORDS were replaying in her head. And along with them, a burgeoning plan. One she hadn't yet shared with Ben or Hale. One that had been there longer than she was ready to admit. It wasn't that she was hiding it. It was more that it had just been secretly growing, quietly and without her permission. And then, like a crafty weed that one day seems to have bloomed into something else… something bold and something with potential — in an instance, she began to see that it was never a weed at all.

The call she'd just made, it was brief. And cryptic. Partially to keep anyone listening in the dark. And partially because she didn't want to lose her nerve in the process. But the person she'd made the call to would understand every word.

Erin continued to walk along the fence that kept Celia's cows. They were off in the distance. She walked through the grass, avoiding mud, and thinking about Celia's words.

"The only thing we can really do is what *we* can do."

That's what Celia had told her. And: there are "things we know in our heart that *need* to be done."

They had no other plans at this point. Nothing that was viable. And right now, everything was stacked against them. The F.B.I. would find them soon. That was a given. And if they didn't have real proof that this was a conspiracy, that Erin was being framed, then it would be game-over. Not to mention, everyone who had helped her along the way — Ben and Hale, for sure, and maybe even Celia — they'd all be tried as accomplices: aiding a fugitive who killed a United States senator.

As she walked, she wondered if she'd made the right decision. Making that call — knocking down an irreversible series of dominoes — without even bringing in Ben or Hale. Even though the focus was on her right now, they were in this, too, just as much.

The sun was getting lower. Turning itself into a fierce shade of orange, gouging the sky around it with deep purple and pink streaks. She stopped walking and looked at the sky. It was long, framing the expanse of Celia's property, all the way to the road leading off the farm.

And then, something else caught her eye.

A car.

But not Hale's Explorer. And not Celia's either.

It had just arrived, there was a cloud of dust around it.

And a person, too.

Waving at her.

No, running toward her.

She squinted her eyes, to make out who it was… It couldn't be… *Gavin?*

38

JONAH

Jonah was riding in the back of one of Eli's cars. He opened up the app on his phone that made his calls secure. With a few taps, he found Eli's contact information and tapped it again to call. He lifted the phone to his ear and waited. The other end gave a soft click, signaling a secure connection was open.

"It's done," Jonah said.

He could hear background noises on the other end. Glasses clanking. A restaurant.

"Well?" Eli said, with no apparent rush in his voice. "Were you successful?"

"Yes."

"Where is she?" Eli said. The two of them, long used to using basic counter-surveillance principles, were careful never to use real names over the phone. Even on a secure line.

"She's willing to meet you," Jonah said.

The line was silent. Jonah couldn't tell if Eli was delaying — one of his endless power games — or just chewing. But if there was one thing he'd learned from Eli over the last thirty years, it was how to play those same power games.

Eli spoke again, slow and measured. "That is not what we agreed to."

"No," Jonah said. "You could send someone. Again. For the... what's this — third time now?"

Eli didn't respond to the sarcasm. "Where does she want to meet?" he said.

"D.C.," Jonah said. "The U.S. Botanical Gardens. Business hours."

"No," Eli said flatly. "Too public."

"Well, that's the point," Jonah said. "You've spooked her. She's on to you now. She can't prove it, yet, but she knows you're the one behind this."

Eli was quiet, and Jonah knew how his gears were turning right now. Jonah was getting to him. Eli could have a United States Senator killed. But now, a *journalist* was attempting to push him into a corner and call the shots. Eli would never be caught saying those words out loud, much less on a phone.

"No," Eli said.

Jonah sighed, not bothering to hide his annoyance.

"We'll do what we did last time," Eli continued. "*It worked.*"

He was talking about sending Val to go after Erin directly, the same way she did for the senator. On lower-profile targets, the standard operating procedure was for someone like Val to hire someone who then hired someone else. That produced a kind of double-blind scenario for assassinations. But it had its risks. It was all for-hire work. No one doing it was invested any more than the money. So in the case of someone high profile, like a U.S. Senator, it was a job Val kept for herself. It was riskier, yes. But it was also much more likely to succeed.

"That's a bad idea," Jonah said.

Eli let out a little laugh at that. "Please," he said. "Enlighten me."

"She's being watched," Jonah said. His tone was short but restrained. Like he was talking to a stubborn child who held an unruly amount of leverage. "If they" — he was talking about the F.B.I. — "put the two of them" — Erin and Val — "in the same place, then it throws shade on the whole narrative. It opens up a new angle in the investigation. And what was, I will admit, well-executed, will now be tarnished."

Eli was quiet for a moment. "We do both," he said finally. "Go along with her little plan. And in the process, execute mine." He was talking about sending Val in his place.

"Not this time," Jonah said. "She's smarter than that. It won't work."

"If I didn't know better," Eli said, "I would begin to wonder about your motives."

"Ha," Jonah laughed. "My motives? My motives are to close this down. Quick and quiet. And," he paused, to get in a jab. "And to not make the same mistake for the third time in a row."

Under all his fluff and his thirst for power, Eli was still a shrewd businessman. And Jonah knew that. He knew how to walk the line, how to get Eli to puff up just enough to realize that prudence — that success — required he pull back a touch. It was an old trick. One Jonah had learned from being on the other side of this same exchange, many years ago. A side effect of having Eli Bren as a father.

"And," Jonah said. "There's something else." He paused, making sure Eli didn't miss this next part. "She knows who you are."

The line was silent for a long moment. This was the tender cherry-on-top. The piece that, if delivered at the wrong time, would be completely steamrolled and lost. Eli had spent his life making and re-making himself. And his past had a touchy habit of popping up at the wrong time. Ruining good, hard-won plan. Jonah could hear the clank of restaurant sounds in the background.

When Eli spoke again, he didn't have any irritation in his voice. He was all business.

"Fine," he said. "I'll meet her. Botanical Gardens. But not during business hours. After. And you" — he paused, "you'll take care of any eyes."

Jonah had anticipated this counter.

And, from his point of view, he didn't want to show up on U.S. Government cameras any more than Eli did. And so he'd already planned to arrange for something along those lines.

Eli spoke again. "We'll do it tomorrow. Midnight. It should be easy enough to do what needs to be done then."

Jonah hung up the phone, without any more words, and let his head fall back onto the headrest behind him. He closed his eyes and took a deep slow breath, letting the air slowly flow back out through his nostrils. He opened his eyes again, looking out at the street as the car continued to drive. He reached down and pushed a button so that the glass between him and the driver slid down. "Take the next right," he said. It had begun. And he had work to do.

39

BACK

Erin saw Gavin standing in the distance, waving. She raised her hand over her eyes, to block out the setting sun. The car that dropped him off was now doing a three-point turn behind him, at the edge of Celia's property, leaving Gavin to walk the long drive. Erin put a hand in the air, a single wave, and wondering how he knew where they were. And…who else might have found out.

She wasn't far from the house. She walked to it, quickly. Going in the side door and down the hall. She bumped into Ben as he was coming out of the bathroom.

"We've got to go," she said.

"What — now?" he said.

"Yeah, now," she said. "Tell Tom."

She didn't wait for his response but instead kept moving, making her way to the room where she'd slept the night before. She pulled together the few things she had, stuffing them in her bag and zipping it up. She looked around, Celia must still be out on the farm somewhere. She made a mental note to find her before they left.

Erin walked outside as Gavin was walking up to the house.

"Hey," Gavin said. His face was bright.

"Gavin," she said. She walked up to him and gave him a short hug. He was carrying a large duffel bag on his back. "I was worried you might have been...," she pulled back and looked at him.

"I think I almost was," he said.

She had a lot of questions she wanted to ask him. Top of the list was how exactly he'd found them. But she told herself she'd have time for all that on the ride back. They had several hours to kill to get back to D.C. And now, since she'd made that call, every minute counted.

"Okay," she said. "I'm glad you're here."

"Me too—" he started.

"But now we're leaving," she said, cutting him off.

"Leaving? I just..."

"I know," she said, turning back to the door she'd just come out of. She pulled it open, without going in, and yelled for Ben again.

Erin let the door close behind her and looked out toward the barn. She saw Hale and Celia walking toward them. She walked back inside and grabbed Hale's keys from the counter. Back outside, Gavin was still standing on the porch next to the door. He'd dropped his bag next to him.

"So, whose place is this?" he asked.

Erin didn't answer him, but instead walked past him to Hale's Explorer, parked around the side. "Bring your bag," she called over her shoulder to Gavin. She walked around to unlock the Explorer. As she did, she could hear Ben walking out of the house and talking to Gavin. At the same time, Hale and Celia walked up.

"What's going on?" Hale said.

"We've got to go. Now," Erin said. "I'll fill you in on the way."

Hale looked around quickly.

"It's not *that*," Erin said. She knew what he was thinking. Wondering if someone had found them here. Or, at least, she hoped it wasn't that. Gavin *had* just found them, of course, but she hoped he was ahead of the curve.

Erin pulled open the back of the Explorer and tossed her bag inside as Hale walked back into the house to get his stuff.

Celia was standing nearby, she brushed her hands on her pants. Erin walked up to her. Celia looked at her and smiled.

Erin wanted to thank her for everything. Not just letting them sleep quietly for a night, off the grid — though she *was* appreciative for that. But there was more. She wanted to explain to Celia what her words had meant. How they'd helped push her in the right direction, just when she needed it. She wanted her to understand all the background in that decision, and all the depth that went with it, so that she could understand what it all really meant. Erin opened her mouth, but only a single "thanks" came out.

Celia put her arms around her and pulled her close, into a hug. Feeling her warmth, it was like she knew everything Erin was thinking, and everything she wanted to say.

Ben and Gavin were walking up behind them.

Celia let her go. "Take care of yourself," she said, lower, so that the rest couldn't hear.

Ben tossed his bag into the back of the Explorer. And Gavin did the same. Hale walked up behind them. He placed his bag in and closed the back of the Explorer.

Erin walked around and got into the backseat. Ben was thanking Celia, while Gavin offered a hasty 'nice to meet you.' Hale waited for Ben and Gavin to get into the Explorer, and then pulled Celia aside to say something to her.

Ben was sitting in the front seat, the same he'd ridden up in. From the back, Erin sat up and reached through the middle, resting her weight on the armrest between the driver and front passenger seats. She put Hale's key in the ignition and started it. She reached to the dash and flipped on the heat.

Still spread between the front and back of the Explorer, her head was close to Ben's. He was looking for the rest of his seat belt, but he stopped and looked at her. In a low voice, meant just for her, he said, "everything okay?"

She pulled her hand away from the heat controls, satisfied for the time being, and rested her weight on her elbows, thinking about that question. "Yes," she said finally. "I think so."

And, she wasn't putting on. Everything was okay. Or, maybe, it was more accurate to say everything was *right*. The world, of course, was falling apart around her. But she was doing what she knew she had to do. And, for the time being, that seemed to be enough. She was doing the right thing. A moment later, Hale got in the driver seat. She sat back and buckled up and they left.

The drive back to D.C. was pleasant. Gavin told them what he'd been up to for the last 24 or so hours. Erin and Ben filled him in on their end. And Hale, typical for him, was quiet for most of the drive. Once in D.C. proper, they found an out-of-the-way motel to stay the night. And as they couldn't go back to Erin's house, they decided to make this their base of operations. At least, for the next day or two. And those days would be critical.

40

DINER

Erin woke up, hearing birds. For a moment, she didn't know where she was. She lifted her head and looked around. Solid white linens piled around her. Cheap artwork on the walls. She let her head drop back on her pillow, closing her eyes. Motel.

The four of them rented two rooms last night. They requested adjacent rooms, with a joining door so that they could open it up and turn it into a workspace during the day. She turned over and looked at the red LED numbers next to her bed. The sun was up, cutting through the cracks in the blinds. But it was still early.

She let out the kind of sigh that comes with an unrestful night of sleep. Turning over, she sat up and got out of bed. She walked to the bathroom and turned on the shower. She felt the water and slipped in. The warmth felt good.

On the drive back, last night, Gavin passed out burner phones. He'd picked them up, cheap, at a Walmart before he left D.C. Simple pre-paid flip phones. They needed a way to communicate that wouldn't be tracked.

When Erin got in last night, after the other three went to her room, she texted Jonah.

It's me. Tomorrow. 7am. The diner.

Even though the phone and the number weren't in any way connected to her or her name, she still wasn't taking chances. Keeping it all vague. As she got out of the shower in the small bathroom, she pulled a white towel off the rack and wiped condensation off the mirror. She picked up the burner phone from the bathroom counter and looked at it.

Still no response.

She put on most of the same clothes she'd been wearing the day before and towel-dried her hair. Back in the main part of her room, she found a book on the dresser with a taxi service's number. She called it, telling the dispatch to meet her a few blocks from where her motel was. Another precaution. She put on her tennis shoes and her jacket. Looking once more in the mirror, she ran her hands through her hair. That would have to do. She grabbed her room key card from the dresser and left, shutting the door softly behind her.

The D.C. winter was getting colder. And the brisk wind felt a bit worse with her still-damp hair. She walked to the door next to hers, bent down and wedged a note through the crack under the door. Letting the guys know she'd be back.

She walked the few blocks to meet the taxi. It had just pulled up, and, from the looks of it, was about to pull away. She flagged it down and got in. The driver inside was wearing a red Santa hat. But that was about the only thing cheery about him. A lot of taxi drivers were losing work these days to ride-sharing companies. When you consider what it actually costs a taxi driver, just in fees alone, to keep the thing legal, it's not a huge surprise so many are turning to easier ride-sharing services. It seemed like mostly just the old battle-axes like this that were left. Guys who'd been driving a cab for thirty years and would probably die driving a cab.

She told him the name of the diner and the cross streets. He knew the place. They were on the beltway now, and she was watching out the back window as they drove. Traffic was almost nonexistent for a workday. *No*, she remembered, not a workday. Today was…

"Is this—" she said to the driver. "Is today… Christmas?"

He adjusted his rearview mirror and looked at her like she'd just escaped from somewhere. He nodded his head slowly. "Yeah. It's Christmas," he said it like it had to be the stupidest question he'd ever heard. And, to his credit, Christmas morning didn't *usually* slip up on people. He pointed to his red hat. As if that should have been proof enough from the start. "You didn't see the hat?" He shook his head and fixed his mirror, saying something else under his breath. *Christmas morning*, she thought.

A few minutes later, the driver pulled up at the diner, the same one she and Jonah had spent half the night talking after he'd— after that man had come after her. It seemed ages ago now. But it had only been two days. Or three. It was all blending together, and she was having a hard time keeping track. She got out of the cab, and it left. She looked down at her watch. Five after seven.

She walked up to the diner and pulled the door open. From somewhere behind the counter, she heard someone telling her to sit anywhere. She quickly scanned the room, her eyes landing on the same booth they sat at last time.

She felt a flutter in her chest.

He was there.

Sitting with a view of the door, she could see his face. But he wasn't looking at her. He was nursing a coffee.

She walked up to the table and sat down. He looked at her.

"You're late," he drawled.

"I know," she said. "Thanks for meeting me."

She was still wearing her jacket. And she noticed that he was wearing a smooth leather jacket with a clean mock turtleneck. He always seemed to have a put-together quality about himself. She thought about her own appearance, wearing the same clothes from yesterday. She'd brushed her hair by running her hands through it. If she were making comparisons, she would feel a little insecure right now.

He was looking at her, in the eyes as he always did, waiting. She opened her mouth, to lay into her plans, when a kid walked up to their table. Not a kid, a teenager. The employee lowest on the ladder, the one who gets stuck with the Christmas morning shift. He launched into one of their specials or something. Erin looked up at him, but Jonah didn't take his eyes off her.

She realized how hungry she was and ordered a full breakfast. And a coffee.

The kid looked at Jonah, waiting for him to order, too. But he didn't acknowledge him. Instead, he continued to watch Erin.

"He's good," Erin said, handing the menu back to the kid.

"Ohh-kay," the kid said, making two clear words out of it.

The kid walked away and Erin filled Jonah in on the rest of her plan.

Jonah was shaking his head. "This is a bad—"

"No," she said, cutting him off.

He stopped talking, more bemused than annoyed at being given an order.

"We're not going there," she said, pushing forward.

He watched her for a long moment before speaking again. "The meeting," he said. "Is set up for tonight. Midnight."

"Midnight?"

He didn't stop to acknowledge her question, but kept talking. "And there will be no cameras or public."

Erin thought about this. The whole idea was to have a controlled, safe place to talk. She wasn't sure she was okay with these changes. In the last few days, she developed a kind of hope for Eli. For… her father. Not that she ever thought things would turn around and become normal. And she certainly didn't expect he would go unpunished, not held responsible for what he'd done. For her mother. And Paul. And the countless others.

But… she had hope. Hope that, maybe she could appeal to him… as his daughter. A daughter he probably didn't know about. And that, maybe she—

Jonah spoke again, cutting off her thoughts. "Hold out your hand," he said.

"What?"

"Your hand," he repeated.

Her hands had been in her lap. She pulled one up, about to show it to him, still not understanding.

"Under," he said.

She reached out a hand, under the table, and felt something cold. Hard. She thought she'd accidentally grabbed one of the table legs at first. Except it moved. Into her hand.

"Keep It," he said.

She felt the weight of it, realizing he'd just handed her a gun. She pulled it close, trying to hide it even though it was already hidden under the table. Her head and eyes darted to the side, looking around nervously, and then back to Jonah, forcing a calm exterior.

"No," she hissed back at him. "I'm not—"

"You don't have to *use* it," he said. "But make sure you *have* it. Understand?"

She nodded yes. She was holding the gun in her lap, between her legs.

At that moment, the kid came again with her breakfast. She was feeling less hungry now. As he was setting the plate down, his gaze landed on the dark metal shape in her lap. Then his eyes darted to hers as the rest of his body slowly came to a halt. The plate he was about to put down was suspended awkwardly between the two of them. Erin realized he'd just seen the gun in her lap. She quickly moved it out of sight, and smiled — one of her features that had gotten her out of more than a few weird spots.

"It's just for safety," she said. "Dangerous city and all that."

He nodded slowly and let the plate down with a thump on the table in front of her.

"Thanks… Kevin," she said, reading his name tag. He's probably around sixteen, she figured. "I had a boyfriend named Kevin one time," she lied. The suspicion and fear on his face began softened a little. After putting her plate down, once he was standing back up, she noticed his shoulders were back a tiny bit more than they had been before. He didn't respond to the comment, but she could tell he was more at ease now.

Kevin was standing there, at their table, nodding.

"Oh," he added. "More coffee?" He'd been holding a full thermos in his other hand the entire time.

"That would be great, Kevin," she said.

He poured it, still nodding, watching her.

"Thanks Kevin," she said, putting a hand out, genuinely concerned he might overflow her mug.

"Oh yes, okay," he said, pulling the thermos back.

He continued to stand there.

"I think we're good," Erin said, with a nod, signaling it was time for him to leave. "Good," he said. "Okay, yes," and he walked away.

She looked back at Jonah.

Almost imperceptibly, he was shaking his head.

"What would you have me do?" she said. "Shoot him?"

He picked up his mug to take a sip of his coffee, and, noticing it was empty, he put it back down again.

"Hmm," she said. "Mine's full." She picked it up and took a sip of her hot full mug. Jonah wasn't the type to be drawn into these little things. But she still felt a small satisfaction inside. He can condescend all he wants. *Her* way worked.

"What's the rest of your plan?" he said, not bothering anymore with the coffee situation.

"Oh," she said. "Um, that's it."

He looked a little bit surprised. It was unnerving, if she were being honest. Jonah didn't look *surprised* too often.

"This...," he said slowly. "Is a terrible idea."

In truth, she hadn't told him *everything*. But... she had told him most of it. And his vote of non-confidence wasn't helping.

"Well," she said. "It's happening whether you like it or not."

He looked at her again. "That is true," he said, dryly.

She started eating. They talked about a few more details. And logistics. But mostly, she thought, as she sat there — across the table again from Jonah Lennox, of all people — she thought about how far she'd come. How far *they'd* come. It was surreal, for sure. Jonah wasn't a simple person. He'd done a lot of bad things in his life, and he didn't feel the need to hide that. Nor did he seem interested in apologizing. But he'd also done some good things. She wasn't yet sure why. And she didn't fully understand why he'd risked his life for her, *twice* now. But, in a kind of way that *wasn't* warm and tingly, the whole thing felt… right.

MOTEL

As soon as Erin arrived back at the motel, from meeting with Jonah, she went to her room. She shut the door quietly behind her and walked straight to her bag, pulling the pistol out from the small of her back, under her jacket, and burying it under her stuff. She pushed it to the bottom of her bag. She would tell the others about it, but not yet. She had *other* things to tell them first.

Someone knocked on the door. It was Ben. She could hear him through the other side. He must have heard her door shut when she came in. She glanced up at the mirror, running her hands through her hair again. "Hang on," she called, fussing with her hair once more before giving up. She took off her jacket and tossed it onto the bed, and taking one last look at her de-jacketed self, walked to the door and opened it up.

Erin didn't tell Ben about her meeting with Jonah until after she'd gotten back. He'd been surprisingly okay with the whole thing. Her meeting with Jonah, by herself. The main reason she kept it a secret was because of the history between Jonah Lennox and the rest. Rafael, she heard from Ben, still harbored a bit of a grudge from being shot by him in Colombia. Understandable. And Hale, even though he'd been suspended from the F.B.I. — and even though he was now *harboring a fugitive* — he was still a g-man, through and through. And on a deep ideological level, he didn't get on well with people like Jonah. People who didn't feel the need to play by everyone else's rules.

Erin was beginning to worry that it may be taking its toll on Hale. That she might be asking too much of him.

Ben and Erin were sitting on her unmade bed. He kept asking her questions. He seemed talkative.

"There's something else I wanted to ask *you*," she said.

"Yeah?" he said, looking at her and leaning forward slightly.

"How's Tom doing?" she asked.

"Oh, Tom…," Ben said, look away, examining the ugly painting on the wall. "He's, eh….he's fine." He said it in a flat, forced kind of way.

"No, I mean, it's not *that*," Erin said, reaching out and touching his hand. Ben looked back at her, and then down at her hand on his. She pulled hers back, thinking maybe that was too much. Wondering why *that* was the gesture her subconscious self chose to pull him back to her.

"It's just," she said, trying to refocus. "You know how he is. He's…"

"Not like us," Ben finished.

"Right," she said.

He was sitting closer to her now. She wanted to touch him again. Maybe for him to touch her. For the briefest moment, her mind flittered to an unbidden image of him reaching over and kissing her. A for-real kiss.

No, she told herself. Not that, not now.

She stood up and walked to the other side of the small motel room. Trying to refocus herself.

"What's wrong?" he said.

"Nothing," she said. "I just need to…" But she didn't know *what* she needed to do. There was something there between them, and she wasn't ready to deal with it yet.

Or was there?

Ben was a charismatic person. People were always drawn to him. She noticed that when she first met him. He was easy-going, and he made people comfortable. Maybe she was just reading too much into this. She pulled the drapes aside and looked out the motel window, at the highway. She wanted to picture them together, to try it out, even if just in her mind, to see if there was any chance it could work.

But not now, she told herself. There was too much else she needed to be focusing on right now.

"Okay," she said, steeling herself. She turned back to look at him. "Are the other two up?"

He nodded and walked over to the door adjoining the rooms. He unlocked her side, revealing another door behind it. The one the other side controlled. He knocked, and after a moment, the other door opened. Erin glanced through the opening, and — seeing a much messier room on the other side — decided hers would be their meeting space.

Other than a single uncomfortable stuffed chair in the corner, there weren't any other seats, meaning the bed would be it. She stood and reached over her bed, stretching the comforter to cover her sheets.

Gavin walked in, and shortly after him, Hale.

Ben sat on the bed, up against the headboard. Gavin sat in the uncomfortable chair, and Hale stood against the dresser, his back to the mirror. Erin sat on the bed, more or less in the middle of them. She told them about her meeting with Jonah this morning. Last night, on the ride back into D.C., she'd told them she had a contact close to Eli Bren. But she hadn't told them *who* it was.

After she'd finished recounting her meeting with Jonah, Gavin let out a long low whistle.

She'd already given Ben the gist of her morning meeting, so this was mostly for the benefit of the other two.

She looked at Hale. He was standing with his arms crossed, looking down.

"Why should we trust him?" Hale said, looking up at her.

She was dreading this question. And Ben, mercifully, hadn't asked it.

Erin *did* trust Jonah. But she wasn't sure why. In fact, she could completely understand Hale's point of view on this. If anyone else told her what she'd just told them, she'd be skeptical, too.

"I don't mean to be insensitive about this," he continued. "But do you think, since you learned that he's your half brother, that could be coloring your judgment? And then, the whole thing with saving you the other night — that could have been a setup to build trust."

"I know," she said. "It could be all of that. I just... I can't explain it. I trust him."

Hale was quiet. Clearly not convinced, but also not willing to push it any further at the moment.

Gavin spoke for the first time.

"What I don't get," he said. "Is... why pick the U.S. Botanical Gardens as a meeting place?"

"To start," Erin said. "It's a place I know well. A few years ago, I did an exposé on a nonprofit that partnered with the Botanical Gardens on a community project. And, not to mention, it's one of the few places open on Christmas day."

Christmas day.

They were all quiet at the mention of that. A weird Christmas, no doubt.

Gavin spoke again.

"Wait," he said. "Isn't a public place *outside* safer than one inside?"

"Not really," Hale said. "Outside feels safer, because it's more open. But it's harder to secure. And it's more susceptible to unseen players."

"Unseen players?" Gavin asked.

"Like extra teams we don't know about. Or snipers."

"Snipers?" Gavin said, sitting up a little bit straighter in his chair.

"Just an example," Hale added, waiving off Gavin's concern.

"That's quite an example," Gavin said, sliding back down.

"I'm just saying, it's—" Hale started, but Ben interjected.

"The important thing to remember," Ben said. "Is that, even if we don't fully *trust* Jonah Lennox, it will be a controlled meeting. We will make that happen."

The four of them continued talking through the logistics. Fleshing out the plan. They settled on a way forward, but it was going to require some setup ahead of time. Ben and Hale would handle that.

By the time they were done planning, it was almost lunchtime.

Hale looked at Ben. "We should get going. We don't have much time."

"Right," Ben said.

Ben got off the bed and began making his way to the adjoining room.

"Um, Ben," Erin said.

He stopped and looked back at her.

"Got a minute?"

"Sure," he said.

She motioned her head toward the door outside, and he followed her out.

JUSTICE

ERIN AND BEN WALKED OFF THE MOTEL PROPERTY, ON the sidewalk next to the highway. There weren't many cars. Ben was wearing a pair of dark jeans and a thin Northface jacket. The sun was bright, and the wind was slicing through them in sheets. It hadn't snowed yet, but it felt like it might be cold enough. Erin pushed her hands deeper into her pockets.

"You're not cold?" Erin said, looking at him.

He smiled. "Nah. This thing's warmer than it looks." He reached out one of his arms and locked it through hers, pulling her closer to him in the process. The two of them walked a little more without talking.

"Thanks for doing all of this," she said finally.

"Erin," he said, looking at her, "I know that's not why you asked me out here."

After a few steps, they were walking mostly in sync. But his legs were longer than hers, and so it wasn't the smoothest way to walk.

"No, it's not," she said. "But I just wanted you to know. I

really do appreciate it." She moved a little closer to him, though she wasn't sure if he could tell.

"And," she continued. "I know what Paul meant to you. He was my mom's cousin, and I remember him when I was growing up, but I never really *knew* him that well. He was always gone, or living overseas. Spending time with people like you," she said, looking at him with a smile.

Ben didn't look back at her. "He was a good man," he said.

"And," Erin said. "I know that he did a lot for you. From everything I read in his files, he really did think a lot of you."

"It was the same for me," Ben said. "We lived and worked together constantly for several years. I—" he paused. "I didn't really have anyone else like him. My own dad — I love him — but… we were never terribly close. In a lot of ways, Paul filled that gap. He was like a dad, in a professional sense. Giving me opportunities I wouldn't have had otherwise. Trusting me when," he laughed, "when he probably shouldn't have."

The two of them kept walking.

"Paul," Ben said. "He… he held life loosely. He didn't take anything for granted. He told me once, he was surprised he lived as long as he did. And," Ben smiled. "When you look back at his life, and all the crazy stuff he was involved in, you kind of start to understand what he meant."

Erin let Ben keep talking. She'd heard him mention his parents before. But he'd never talked about them the way he talked about Paul. Erin had never been much of a talker herself, more of an internal processor. But she knew, for a lot of people, getting it out was an important part of the letting-go process.

"Ben," she said. "There's something else you should know about Paul. Something I only recently learned."

He looked at her as they walked. She kept her eyes on the ground in front of her, continuing to talk. "Remember how I told you about what happened to me in Trinidad, those years ago?"

"Of course," Ben said.

"I…," she started and stopped. "I thought I was going to die. No, I *was* going to die," she corrected. "Statistically, kidnappings like that usually don't end well. But," she shook her head. "Someone stepped in. And… stopped it." She took a deep breath as she talked. "And I never found out who they were. Until last week."

She looked up at Ben.

"It was Paul. I read it in his notes."

"Paul?" Ben said. "How did he even know you were there?"

The two of them turned down a corner, making the block. She looked back down, smiling as she thought about it.

"I guess," she said. "He was just keeping tabs on me. He must have known I was investigating Mom's death. And he apparently knew the risk. Clearly more so than I did."

"You told me," Ben said. "That the man you found outside the room you were being held in, that he was killed."

"Yeah," she said. "Maybe that's why he never mentioned it," she shrugged.

The two continued to walk, letting that idea settle between them. And other memories of Paul, too. Then Erin stopped walking and pulled her arm away from Ben's. She turned and looked at him. He stopped and returned the look.

"Ben," she said. "If we do this right, we can finish a lot of things today. We can finish what Paul started. And what my mom started." She was thinking about all the corruption Eli

Bren had been involved in. All the people he'd hurt and been responsible for killing over the years.

Ben was nodding slowly. "Justice," he said.

"Justice," she repeated.

43

HER NAME IS ERIN REED

Erin and Ben walked back to the motel. Hale was in his own room, sitting quietly. Gavin was still in the uncomfortable chair in Erin's room, except it looked like he'd made a breakfast run. He was buried in his computer and earbuds.

Erin shut the door behind her and slipped off her jacket, tossing it onto the bed. Ben walked through the door connecting the two rooms, over to his side, where Hale was. Erin's TV was on silent in the background.

She didn't have her computer with her. That was part of everything else she'd left, not realizing she wouldn't be able to return to her house. Probably for the better, though, she thought. If they were tracking her, her computer would be a liability. She grabbed a pad of motel stationery from the dresser and pushed off her shoes. She climbed onto the bed, sitting cross-legged against the headboard. She began writing a list of people she'd need to reach out to soon.

Part of the plan was, with hard evidence in hand — or hard evidence eminently coming — to reach out to a group of strategic allies. But it all had to be last-minute. Hale advised her on the time she'd have to do this. And it wasn't much. If she reached out too early, her list of allies would become a list of accomplices. And not only would she be sending the F.B.I.'s scrutiny their way, but any evidence she collected in the meantime would likely be tainted by her fugitive status, causing it to quickly lose its effect. Or, at the very best, be delayed while she was prosecuted. And given the nature of who they were up again, that was as good as not having the evidence at all.

She thought about Conall McGillis, her editor at the *Post*.

She had a big ask coming his way. She was going to send him recordings. Recordings she didn't yet have. And she was going to need him to write up the story and get it published within a few hours. The writing wasn't the hard part. With over thirty years under his belt, he could write articles like this in his sleep. It was the corroboration she'd be asking him to forego. One of the top commandments in journalism was to verify. The old saying *trust, by verify* came from the world of reporters. You don't have to *name* your additional sources, but you better be sure to have them. It's unthinkable to float a story — especially one of this magnitude — without anyone else confirming that it's legit. And that was exactly what she'd be asking him to do.

But it wasn't only that. With an organization like the *Washington Post*, nobody had immunity. Even McGillis. If this blew up in a bad way, his job and reputation would be on the line.

The alternative, she thought, was still worse.

Everything about her plan had to do with timing. The only real advantage she had over Bren was to catch him off guard. To get the information she needed and to make it public before he could do anything.

Erin looked up, thinking, when something on the TV caught her attention.

Her picture.

She bolted up, jumping off the bed, dropping the memo pad in the process.

"Where's the remote?" she said to Gavin in a half-yell.

"Huh?" he said, pulling his earbuds out, looking up at her.

"The remote," she said — her hand was out and her eyes were stuck on the screen.

"It's…," he started, about to say "here." But he stopped. He was holding out the remote, frozen, as he too saw her picture on the TV screen. It was a breaking news segment.

"Turn on the volume," she said.

"Oh right," he said, looking down, pushing buttons on the remote.

Ben walked back in. "What wrong?" he said. And then, looking at the TV, he froze.

The sound was on now and the news anchor was talking.

"The F.B.I. has released their primary suspect," the anchor was saying. "In the murder of Senator Avery Cleason. Her name is Erin Reed. If anyone has any information on her whereabouts, you are urged to call the F.B.I.'s information hotline."

Erin's face — a still from the security camera in the Dirksen Senate Office building, from when she went to visit Cleason the night he died — was plastered on the TV next to the news anchor.

Erin sat back down on the edge of the bed, still watching the anchor, but no longer listening.

Gavin swore, the word coming out in slow motion.

Hale walked in, joining the rest of them, and watched the TV.

"This is bad," he said.

Erin looked up at him, but didn't really see him. She looked back at her picture on the TV.

It felt like the four of them were suspended, temporarily existing outside of time, as the news anchor continued to break the news that Erin was the primary suspect in the Cleason murder. They all knew she was on the F.B.I.'s radar. But making it public, that changed things. That was a new level. And whatever plan they were *about* to float…it had just been sunk.

●
44

GUARD SHACK

JONAH STOOD WITH HIS BACK AGAINST THE EDGE OF THE gigantic tropical section. The Conservatory at the Botanical Gardens was a sweeping indoor series of rooms, designed to preserve all kinds of plants, year-round. And the tropical section was hot. Jonah was holding a tourist pamphlet. In front of him, at a diagonal, across the way, were the medical plants. And in his perfect line of sight was the security room. He'd been watching the old man, on and off for two days now. The primary job of security during the night was to make sure homeless people didn't slip in. During the day, the security was much heavier, but Jonah figured that was more about appearances.

The old man's shift had just started. Jonah had been in the security room once before, yesterday. Mostly it was to scope out the equipment. He needed to stop the security cameras from setting off alarms. In the movies, they'd use some mysterious little gadget with a mini video feed monitor, and they'd clamp it onto an ethernet cable or something. That would magically switch the security feed into the safe pre-recorded one. Unfortunately, that sort of thing was pure fantasy. In real life, security system companies had seen all those moves. And if you were going to get around them, you had to think outside of the box. Look for the point of failure. And for this system, that point of failure was the arthritic old man monitoring it. The system itself wasn't a bad one. The good news was that it was widely used. And so its documentation was easy to find online. After reading through it, Jonah realized the plan was simple. Switch the feed to review mode. It would essentially allow you to playback a previous recording. And since, after closing, the old man would be the only person in the entire building — and since absolutely nothing would change on the screens from night to night — Jonah was going to use the previous night's footage. He'd slip in, set the system to review mode, and then slip back out. Everything would look like it always did. The only area that might tip the old man would be the timestamp. If he looked closely, he'd see yesterday's date. But Jonah didn't think that would be a problem. There would be no reason for him to even look.

Jonah looked up, the sky beyond the enormous glass ceiling was dark. The soft interior lights around him had come on. He looked at his watch. According to yesterday — and the old man's arthritis — he does just two rounds. One when he first gets on his shift, which should happen in a few minutes. And then one, just after closing time, to ensure everyone leaves.

The painted green metal door to the security room opened. Jonah kept his head down, reviewing his brochure. As the old man moved through the door, he let it close behind him as he walked on. The door made a squeak on its hinges, but the latch that closed and locked it behind him was well oiled, making the final movement of the door silent. That would work, Jonah thought.

The old man hobbled past where Jonah stood. He made eye contact, nodding a silent hello as he passed.

First round.

Jonah waited until he was gone. He was standing in an area just outside of any of the cameras. Soon, he'd reposition to another non-camera point close by to wait. Before the old man's final round and just after closing time, he'd find a spot out of sight, very close to the green security door. Close enough that, when the old man walked out and let it shut behind him, he could catch the door. Just after it squeaked and just before it locked. The man would make a ten minute round. Jonah would need two minutes, at most.

45

SURVEILLANCE

Erin was standing, arms crossed, watching her own face on the motel TV.

"This… changes things," Hale said.

"No," Erin turned around. "No, it doesn't."

Ben lifted his hand, pointing at the TV. "You just became America's most wanted."

"It's Eli Bren," she said, looking back at the TV. "He's behind this."

And he was. Erin knew it. She'd done her research on Eli Bren. And combined with what Paul had collected, she knew some of the things he's set up in the past. And, not to mention, he was well connected in Washington. It wasn't that he was running a scam. The F.B.I. couldn't be bought off like that. But the right people could be influenced. That was just psychology 101. And if you were in a position to do that, then they were as much as at your disposal. Bren was about to be awarded a gigantic Defense department contract. He'd already been vetted. And, according to what the Pentagon was screening for, he'd come up clean. But then again, how many corrupt politicians were in the same boat.

Gavin spoke. "What does that mean?" he asked. "You think he's trying to keep you from coming tonight?"

Erin thought about that. She knew this was Bren. It had to be. But she didn't understand the play. It wouldn't — unless...

She walked up to the TV and reached up, turning it off. She turned back to the others. "I don't know if he had control over the timing," she said. She was talking calmly. Calmer than she expected herself to be right now. "But it plays into his favor."

The three of them were watching her.

"He knows I have something on him. Something good. Otherwise he wouldn't agree to meet. Wouldn't even entertain it."

Hale was looking down, nodding along as she talked.

"But the last thing a man like that wants is to be caught over the barrel. Especially by someone like me. Someone he's clearly more powerful than." She was moving her hands now, as she talked. It was as if the blow — becoming a public enemy — had only served as fuel. "You see," she said. "He needs me to feel desperate. To go to the meeting and agree to whatever terms he gives me. Because I won't have any other choice."

Ben was sitting on the bed, watching her talk. "But...?" he said.

She knew she had a chance. And she needed everyone playing their part along the way if it was going to work. Eli Bren would fall. But it was a precarious bridge she'd need to walk to make him fall. And one that, if she wasn't careful, could easily bring her down, too.

"But we're not going to do that," she said.

She stopped talking and the other three were quiet.

Hale looked up at her. "This," he said, waving at the now dark TV, "leaves us a bit exposed. Everything is shortened.

It's different. More people will be looking for you now. And the timelines, they'll all be shortened too…"

"Wait," Gavin said.

Erin, Ben, and Hale looked at him.

"There's a Micro Center — on the way to the Botanical Gardens."

"So?" Hale said.

"What's a Micro Center?" Ben said.

"It's like a modern Radio Shack," Gavin said. "They sell portable, closed-circuit surveillance systems."

Erin was beginning to understand. Gavin had been quiet. But he'd been problem-solving. The compressed timeline Hale was talking about wasn't just a reference to law enforcement's efforts. It meant that the public and the media would have very little patience for any kind of investigation once Erin was caught. Meaning, they'd need to have rock-solid evidence. There was no room for ambiguity or speculation. It had to be immediately convincing.

"Do it," she said, looking at Gavin.

Hale looked down at his watch. "We need to go," he said. "Now."

Gavin closed his laptop and slid it into his duffel bag. He stood up, hefting it over his shoulder. Closest to the door, he opened it. The cold outside air blew in. The sky was almost completely dark now. Gavin was already outside. Hale was standing next to the door. Ben next to him. Erin walked back to her bag, to grab something. She turned, about to follow the rest out.

Ben stopped, between her and the door.

"What?" she said.

"Erin," he said, letting out a sigh. "You should probably stay here."

"What do you mean?"

"We need to keep you off the grid as long as possible." He looked outside and then back her. "If anyone sees you…"

She looked down, at the ugly patterned carpet.

He was right.

Ben continued to watch Erin. "I'll call you," he said. "As soon as we're in place."

Hale reached down and pulled a small pistol from a holster at his ankle. He pulled out the little magazine, checked it, and slipped it back in. He replaced it in his ankle holster, fixing the leg of his jeans at the bottom. "We need to go," he said, looking at Ben. He walked out of the open door, leaving Ben and Erin in the room.

The cold air was flowing into the room.

"Okay," Erin said, nodding, not looking at Ben. "Fine."

Ben reached down and grabbed one of her hands. She looked up at him. He didn't stay anything else. He squeezed her hand and let it go. "Talk soon," he said.

And with that he walked out, shutting the door behind him. She looked around at the dead quiet motel room. It was just her now. She could hear Hale's Explorer outside starting up. She sat on the edge of the bed. Looked at her watch. And then looked around the room again. All she had to do now was wait.

46

DRY RUN

Val sat on a metal bench, its iron-work making an uncomfortable floral pattern in her back. She could smell a faint sweetness from the flowers behind her. Flowers she'd never seen before.

Jonah was on the other side of the conservatory. She knew that. Eli knew that. But she wasn't sure yet if he knew she was here. The shift, she'd noticed, had been almost palpable in the last several months. Eli no longer trusted Jonah. He still used him, yes. But trust him, no. And that's why Val was here. To make sure things ran smoothly. She didn't know the details of the meeting. Nor, honestly, did she really care. But Eli was nervous about it for some reason. Not that he told her that. But she was good at picking up on those details.

She breathed in deeply, mouth closed, letting the air slip slowly out of her nose.

An old man hobbled her way. He was wearing navy, top to bottom, with a utility belt and a radio clipped to it. There was a small badge on his chest. Security. She watched him walk. He favored his right leg. Probably a very old injury made worse by age. Catacorner to where she sat was a long shallow pool, with a walkway on either side.

The old man walked by her on the bench. As he did, he gave her a smile and a nod. She smiled back, warmly. He was walking close to the pool as he made his rounds.

She looked quietly in the way he'd come. For the moment, there was no one else around.

She stood up, slipped off her flats and walked barefoot after him. Without shoes, she didn't make a single sound.

The old man continued to walk on. He didn't look at the plants. Or anything. He just walked. Like he'd done this a thousand times before. Which, he probably had.

As he continued to walk, he moved closer to the shallow pool, walking around a plant.

And so did Val.

She looked down at the water, as they walked by. If he looked down, he might see her reflection. She was about fifteen feet behind him now. The pool, she looked down again, had probably twelve inches of water in it. Deep enough.

She closed the distance between her and the old man in a few steps. Like a gazelle. Just behind him, she made a small sound. But it wasn't an accident. It was enough for him to stop and turn.

But he didn't finish the movement.

She planted one of her feet right next to his. Her pinstriped business skirt rode up just enough to give her the motion she needed to move. And then, with more strength than her slender frame looked capable of, she grabbed his utility belt with one hand. He was too heavy for her to lift him off the ground. But she pulled, and it was enough force to disrupt his balance. With her other hand, still pulling on his belt, still with her foot planted next to his, she pushed his shoulder blade. Hard. Losing his balance, his foot tripped over hers and did the rest of the work.

And he fell, face down, with an echoing splash into the pool.

He was near the edge. But before he could bring his head back up, she pushed her barefoot down hard, in between his shoulder blades. Other than her foot, she didn't even have to get wet. Her full weight was on his back now. Holding him down. His arms moved, but it didn't matter. She didn't look around. She just stared at the back of his head. It kept moving. And then, after another minute of this, it stopped. His arms floated out to the side. And she put her other foot back onto the ground next to the pool. He'd be discovered tomorrow. A drowning accident.

Except it wasn't.

The old man… he wasn't in the water.

He was still walking along at his uneven pace, still favoring his right leg.

And Val hadn't just followed him and held him under until he stopped moving.

Though she could have. In her mind it was so real. And so easy. Almost not even a challenge — even *with* the people who were still around.

No, she still sat on her bench, continuing to watch the old man walk away. Down at the end, he turned the corner, put up a hand, waving to someone out of sight, and continued to hobble along.

Val turned her head and looked the other way. She took another long slow breath in. It was helpful to visualize these sorts of things. It took away the variables, for when it would *actually* happen. And, sometimes, she was just ready — itching to do it. And the fantasy released her. At least, for the time.

She looked to the other side of the conservatory, to where

Jonah was. She didn't trust his loyalties. But he was competent. Despite what Eli said, Jonah was very good at what he did. Val wouldn't kill the old man. Not yet anyway. She'd let Jonah's plan play out a bit further. He might need the old man for something else. And that was fine. But soon, the time would come, and all that would be done. And when it did, if Jonah didn't do what needed to be done — and a part of her hoped he wouldn't — then she most certainly would.

Still sitting on the metal bench, she caught another waft of the sweetness from the flowers behind her. And she closed her eyes. She put her hand around the edge of the seat. And with a tug, it moved. It was heavy. She thought of another scenario. Life was abundant with those.

She opened her eyes again as a young family walked by. A mom and dad, looking at the exhibits, reading the plaques, oblivious to the little one below them. She must have been three, maybe four. She'd been hanging on her mother's leg. She stopped and looked up at Val. And then, she slipped back by her mother's leg, her shield. There she was, not hidden. And then she slipped her head back out. Val was watching her. The little girl smiled.

Val watched her for a long moment. And then, she smiled back. Just a little.

The girl disappeared again behind her mother's leg. As if she'd just realized Val was a real person. She peaked her little head around again. Playing now. Val casually looked the other way, and then, cutting her eyes back, looked at the little girl. The girl hadn't taken her eyes off Val, watching her carefully. When she realized she'd been caught, she disappeared again, behind her mother's leg, giggling.

An announcement sounded over the loudspeaker and the family started walking again, shewing the little girl along with them. The little girl, still playing, had already forgotten about the woman sitting on the bench.

47

SET UP

Ben, Hale, and Gavin pulled up to the U.S. Botanical Gardens. It was basically a museum filled with plants. And with no admission cost. They walked inside, passing a woman sitting at the front desk.

"We're about to close," the woman called out to them.

"Thanks," Ben said. "Just a quick trip in and out," he lied.

She didn't seem bothered by this. D.C. was filled with tourists. And the Gardens were on the grounds of the United States Capitol, the most iconic building in D.C. Ben figured people did this all the time.

But still, they weren't taking any chances. Ben and Hale made sure to block most of the woman's view of Gavin. On the trip over, with the stop off at the Micro Center, he'd downsized his duffel bag to a backpack. And it was currently filled with small portable CCTV security cameras. Ben was pretty sure bags were allowed inside. But he was also pretty sure the contents of *their* bag wasn't.

The three of them walked inside. The inside opened up around them. It was huge.

"This is…uh," Gavin said, looking around. "Bigger than I expected."

"Let's go," Hale said.

Ben grabbed a map from a stand near the entrance. He looked at it as they walked. The conservatory was essentially a big square. There were snaking paths winding throughout it. And it was divided, mostly, by the kind of plants in each section.

"We'll need good lighting," Gavin said. "For the cameras to pick up faces."

The place was currently well lit, but Ben figured a bit of that would be turned off once the place was shut down.

"Here," Ben said, pointing to a spot on the map. "The canopy walk. That's going to be a big open space. Let's start there."

Hale glanced at it as he continued to walk. The three of them moved farther into the Gardens. As they did, Gavin was looking around, scouting locations to plant their cameras.

"We've only got a few cameras," he said. "So we need to put them where we'll get the maximum exposure."

Ben was looking around. He'd been a photographer for years. And this was not ideal lighting. He figured it would only get worse once it was officially closed for the night.

"How well can these cameras see in the dark?" Ben asked Gavin.

"Somewhat. But that's usually for motion. We still need pretty good light if they're going to be worth anything to us."

"How about that?" Hale said, pointing up toward the canopy walk. It crossed over the large open middle, giving a wide view of the place. Gavin looked up at. "That might work," he said. "I'm going to go check it out."

Ben nodded as Gavin walked toward the canopy. He and Hale continued to walk on the ground level. They were near a long shallow pool now. A woman — whose face Ben didn't see — was sitting at a bench nearby. She was wearing a dark skirt and blouse. But she stood up and walked away before they got close. She walked down one of the narrow paths. Probably leaving, Ben thought, looking down at his watch. The place was almost empty. As they walked farther in, they passed a young family going in the opposite direction.

Over the loudspeaker, they heard the last call. Closing time.

"Come on," Ben said, his voice lower.

He and Hale slipped out of the main area to find a place to hide. They'd let the place close, let the staff leave, and then they'd resume their setup work. They still had a few hours before Erin was set to meet with Eli Bren. It should be enough time to do everything they needed to.

But Ben — normally cool under these kinds of situations — had a feeling he couldn't shake. A feeling like something was… off.

48

CLOSE

Erin closed the motel door behind her. There was an ominous feel in the air. Walking outside after having seen your name and face broadcast on national TV as the suspect in a murder investigation. She looked around, as if expecting to be ambushed, or found out. As if the whole world were watching and waiting to pounce.

As the door clicked shut, nothing but the cold December wind seemed to know she was out there.

She pulled her jacket tighter and started walking. Earlier, out of her boredom, or maybe because of it, she'd been checking and re-checking her interview recorder. Testing it. Making sure it worked. Making sure the mic picked up at a good volume even when it was buried in her pocket. Or, making sure she could turn it on without taking it out and making a show of it. Right around the one-hundredth time she'd turned it on and off again, she noticed the little red light on the side come on. It wasn't the power light. This particular digital recorder didn't have a light for that. It meant the batteries were low. She looked down at her watch.

It wasn't all bad news. She still had a few hours. And she had been itching to do something. To get out. She'd make a battery-run, quick and quiet, and save her sanity in the process.

She was walking along the sidewalk, the same one she and Ben had walked earlier in the day. Except, now she didn't have the sun's warmth. Or Ben's. She put her head down and kept walking. Cutting some of the cold wind. She looked up briefly and crossed the street. She remembered seeing a convenience store a few blocks away. She closed her eyes as she continued to walk. The wind was biting. As she walked, she thought about what was coming. Being in her hotel room, where they'd talked through the plan, it still felt hypothetical. A concept. Not reality. Not yet. But now, being out, and being alone, the weight of it was beginning to rest on her. Now, her plan was beginning to seem ridiculously fragile.

The long and short of it all was to use her connection to Eli Bren, as his daughter — something she was pretty sure he may have had suspicions about, but no proof — and then get him talking about what he'd done. Hale was there to call it in. Not to the local police. But to his boss in the Bureau. He'd also call the locals — that would get sirens and lights in the area, quickly. But first, he'd call Mick, his F.B.I. boss. Mick could run it up the chain, cutting through the red tape and saving a lot of time. With Erin's current state as public enemy number one, calling just the cops only would be a disaster. Mick — with the right evidence — would understand and know what to do.

Erin and Gavin, from the technical side, would essentially be doing the same thing. Only his would be a bit more advanced. They'd be recording Eli Bren. But there were more than a few points of failure here. Erin knew the Botanical

Gardens pretty well. But Gavin didn't. And he'd have to get in, set up, and make sure the whole thing worked. She'd told him where they'd likely be meeting. There were only a few potential spots inside. And part of her job for the night was to make sure Eli picked the right one. She didn't really think she'd be able to get away with recording the whole thing herself. What if they searched her? But maybe they wouldn't.

She kept walking. Her recorder was still in her pocket. And, as a nervous habit, she kept turning it on and off. In the last couple hours, she'd gotten pretty good at doing that on the sly. In the past, it was never a skill she needed. A lot of states required a two-party consent to record. Meaning, both the recorder and the recordee need to be on board for it to be legal. And besides, most sources frowned on being recorded without their knowledge. So she'd typically had the thing on the table between them, making it clear what was happening. That would be the very opposite of what she'd be attempting in a few hours.

She walked up to the corner store. Its blue-green fluorescent lights contrasted hard against the yellow streetlight outside. The automatic door slid open and she walked in. The place had the feeling of being both sterile and dirty at the same time. The way convenience stores sometimes are. But, mercifully, it was a haven from the wind and the cold. She felt her body relax a little as she walked in, scanning the aisles for batteries. Picking up a pack, she began walking to the counter up front.

She hadn't considered this before, but now, walking up to the counter, she was getting nervous.

She put the batteries on the counter, not making eye contact.

"That all for you?" the clerk said.

"Yeah," Erin said, still not looking at the woman behind the counter. She reached in her pocket, realizing she didn't have any cash, only a card. Anything trackable was off-limits right now. And that included credit cards. But, if everything went according to plan, this would all be over soon. She chanced it, figuring it would be at least a day until one of her credit cards set off alarms. Plenty of time… she hoped. She pulled out her card and waited.

But the clerk had stopped working.

Erin turned away, casually, looking at the Christmas decorations in the store, as if they were interesting enough to keep her attention all this time. She wanted to look at the clerk. To see why she'd stopped ringing her up. But that was just paranoia, she told herself. Most people didn't watch the news anyway, and she—

"Hey," the clerk said.

Erin turned and looked at her.

She'd been holding Erin's batteries over the bag, her hand was frozen in the middle of its motion. "Aren't you…," she started. Her other hand was pointing to a small TV, behind the counter.

"No," Erin said quickly.

"It's funny," the clerk said with a little laugh. "Because you look just like that woman on the news. The one that killed the senator or something."

"Huh," Erin said. "Weird." She handed her the credit card, to get the whole process moving again.

The clerk took it, looking down at the name on it, and then her other hand idly dropped the batteries into the plastic bag.

"Wait a minute…," the clerk said. "What was the name of that person? It was Reed," she said, looking at Erin now. And her eyes were bigger. But less in the horror sense. And more in the here-come-my-fifteen-minutes sense.

"Just an unfortunate coincidence," Erin said, trying to be as casual as she could. She nodded toward the bag with her batteries in it, trying to prompt the clerk again, to keep moving. But it was too late. The woman had discovered something. Something good. And she wasn't going to let it go. Before Erin knew it, she'd pulled out her phone and pointed it at her.

"What are you doing?" Erin said.

The woman didn't answer. She'd taken a picture of Erin and she was typing something into her phone.

"Facebook," the clerk said, without looking up.

"Are you kidding me," Erin said.

"Wait—" the clerk said, looking up. She'd stopped tapping on her phone. And her expression had changed, as if she'd just realized something new. "You're not... like... dangerous or anything... are you?"

The clerk was backing up now. As if, in her mind, she's just connected "wanted for murder" and "dangerous." She grabbed the phone on the counter. The store landline. The strange greed she'd had a moment before was now replaced with real fear. Fear that Erin might "do something."

"It's not me," Erin said, a bit more forceful than she'd meant to.

The woman was holding the store phone to her chest. Erin was pretty sure she was about to call 911. "Come on," Erin said. "Can you please just finish checking me out. It's Christmas Day, and I need to get back to my family," she lied.

But the mention of family only seemed to make things worse. As if the clerk was now thinking about her own family. And being cornered, by a murderer, and all that.

"Oh for—" Erin said. She grabbed the plastic bag of batteries, realizing she was never going to be able to pay for them — or leave if she didn't act now. And with that, she walked quickly out of the store. She knew she was leaving her credit card. But, at this rate, she'd have to go behind the counter to get it. And even then, the clerk was a bit bigger than her. And ready to defend her life, apparently. Erin didn't want to get into any of that. On the way out, she could hear the clerk pounding the numbers on the phone's keypad and yelling something into it.

49

THE BREAKDOWN

GAVIN COULD SEE BEN AND HALE FROM HIS VANTAGE point. They were crouched down, waiting. An old man dressed like an employee had already gone by, probably checking to see that everyone from the day had cleared out after closing time. Gavin looked at the time. Two hours to go. He put his bag on the floor in front of him and pulled out a few portable security cameras. He'd left everything non-essential in Hale's Explorer. The packaging, the manuals, everything that wasn't strictly needed to make them work. Only the cameras, their batteries, the mounting clamps, and a handful of SD cards. He didn't anticipate having time to set the cameras up on a network. Setting up his own network would take equipment he didn't have. And hacking into the Garden's network, without being noticed, would take time he didn't have. So he opted for the simpler option. Each camera had an SD card slot in it. It allowed you to record to local storage, on the device itself. It would mean they'd have to go back and collect each card afterward. But it was a quick and stable solution.

He mounted one of the cameras, checked its vantage

point, and then popped an SD card in. He pushed a button on the side and a green recording light came on.

He'd already installed one a few minutes ago. This install made two. Only eight more to go.

Erin had given him a pretty good idea of where the meeting would happen. She reasoned it would need to be in an open space, to give Eli enough room to feel like he wasn't trapped. And, considering all the little nooks and paths this place had, there weren't enough cameras in the entire Micro Center store — nor enough hours — to cover every angle of this place. So, hopefully she was right.

Gavin zipped his bag and slung it over his shoulder. He was on the canopy walk, hidden from view from anyone below. He took another glance down at Ben and Hale before moving on. He'd find them again later, after he'd finished setting up. As long as he stayed quiet, the old man wouldn't notice him.

But as he looked down at them, he realized something was wrong.

They weren't crouched down like they were before. They were standing. Looking at someone else.

Gavin watched, his heartbeat picking up the pace.

Ben was lifting his hands now.

Gavin's first thought was the old man. The security guard had found them. But a moment ago, he was going in the opposite direction. Gavin looked around, to the other side of the canopy bridge. He couldn't see the old man. He looked back at Ben and Hale. Gavin moved quietly, staying low, to get a better view. He walked behind some plants, and then, from there, he could see better what was going on.

There was a third person.

But it wasn't the old man.

It was… a woman.

And… she was holding a gun, pointing it at Ben and Hale.

Gavin swore under his breathe and quickly dropped back behind cover. He was sitting on the floor against a gigantic orange pot. His breath was coming fast now. He pushed himself up, looking again over the edge, where the three of them were.

The woman was taking Ben and Hale away somewhere.

Gavin slipped back down, closing his eyes. "This is not good," he said to himself, trying his best not to hyperventilate. "This… is not good."

50

TIED

BEN MOVED TO THE SIDE AS HALE TOOK THE HIT. THE two of them were sitting in a windowless room, shoulder to shoulder, tied down. The woman in front of them looked more like a corporate lawyer.

But Ben knew who she was. And she wasn't that.

Valentina Dias.

She wasn't on many law enforcement radars. From what he'd read, she was very good at staying off of them. Up until a month ago, he'd only seen her once or twice, and just from surveillance photos. After Erin looked through Paul's research, she filled him in on who this woman was. Paul had been working for her in Colombia, gathering intel.

The thought of Paul brought a knot to his throat. The work he'd been doing, he called it *Vesper*. The last prayer. He must have always known he'd go down before this whole thing did.

Another crack jerked Ben back to the present. The butt of her gun connected with Hale's face.

Ben looked at Hale, tied next to him. His face was bloody, and hanging down. But he was still awake. And to his credit, he hadn't said a word since she'd grabbed them. And… to Ben's confusion, the woman had focused all of her attention on Hale, leaving him largely untouched.

She hit Hale again.

Ben felt the rock of Hale's body, push against his. Little warm drips landed on his face. Hale's blood.

"Stop," Ben said. "Just… stop it."

She was standing in front of them, her hand holding her pistol by the barrel. The way she'd been using it, as a club, Ben could see red smears on the end of its silver handle. She turned and looked at Ben. She was breathing like she'd just run up a flight of steps. But there was something else. Something more dangerous than the physical blows…. she seemed to be…. enjoying it. A grin slipped across her open mouth.

"Do *you* want my attention now?"

She took a step to the side, saying the words slowly. She was standing more in front of Ben.

Ben, for his part, was doing his best not to show the fear that was mounting inside of him. He was breathing through his nose. But his mouth was getting dry.

"What do you want?" he said. His voice sounded a bit more pathetic than he'd hoped for.

"Thomas Hale and Ben Okello," she said, pointing with the butt of her pistol, to each of them as she said their names. "I have exactly what I want."

Ben let out a breath. He realized he'd been holding as she talked.

"Why?" he said.

She didn't answer him. Her grin turned into a smile. And then, without warning, she turned around and walked out of the room. Ben could see her pulling out her phone, tapping into it and then holding it to her ear. He could hear her talking, but he could not make out any of the words. At one point, she looked back at him as she talked into her phone.

Ben turned his head and looked at Hale next to him. He could tell he was having a hard time staying conscious. He wanted to tell him to hang on. To say to him something optimistic, to keep his spirits up. But Ben couldn't think of anything. Gavin was out there. If he was lucky, he'd find a way to get out before this woman caught him. Maybe, if he did, he could warn Erin. Warn her that she was walking into an ambush.

He thought about Erin. He wasn't holding out any hope for himself and Hale making it out of this. He closed his eyes tight, as he realized, he probably wouldn't see her again. Whatever this woman would do to him next, it would be nothing compared to that. Realizing he would not see Erin again seemed to hurt more than anything else.

His eyes burned as he kept them shut. He held them so tight he began to see a kaleidoscope of stars. And then, he thought about Paul. About all he'd done. For him personally, but giving his life to make this thing right. Ben felt the tiniest bit of strength at that.

He looked up again. He knew what was coming. And he couldn't stop it.

But he wouldn't be afraid of it.

51

JONAH

Jonah looked down at the screen on his phone. It was Val. He tapped the button to answer.

"What," he snapped.

"Were you going to tell me?" She said it in her sing-song kind of way.

"Tell you what?"

"About their little plan."

Jonah sighed, not bothering to hide it. "I don't have time for games, Val. What is this about?"

"The two lurkers. The F.B.I. one and the black one. I found them. Inside."

Jonah was quiet. Thinking.

He and Erin had agreed on a plan. She was going to coax a confession out of Eli. Jonah thought that was supremely naive — and he told her the same. But she was adamant. For his part, he was clear: the meeting could only be the two of them. Him and her. Anyone else was a variable. And the more variables, the less he could control. Eli, he warned her, was not someone you could leave anything to chance.

And now there was this.

She'd broken the plan.

But, he thought, that wasn't entirely fair. There was a bit of the plan that he'd never told her about. The part about her being bate. He didn't think she'd have any chance of getting a real confession out of Eli. That's not why he agreed to be here tonight. The truth was, he wasn't *really* helping her. He was using her. Eli had agreed to this meeting — probably, he wanted to hear, first hand, what she knew. And then, when he was satisfied, he'd have Val kill her. It was as simple as that. Jonah knew how it would go down. He'd known for too many years how it always went down.

She was a pawn.

But, in a strange way, she also wasn't. There was… something else. Despite himself, he was a bit impressed with her. She had a certain kind of spunk. No real chance in *this* fight. She was too sloppy for that. Too trusting. But there was something there — something he wasn't quite ready to admit to himself about her. Something he liked.

But it didn't matter.

It would all be over after tonight. Jonah wasn't playing Eli's game. Not anymore. Tonight, he was playing one of his own. And now, he'd finally do what he should have done all those years ago. To people like Erin, Eli Bren was evil. Jonah had different ideas about evil. He'd done enough "evil" over the years that that kind of label wasn't helpful. No, for Jonah, it was just math. Eli had taken too much.

And tonight Jonah would stop him from taking anything else.

And he'd do it. Himself.

"Jonah—" Val said.

Jonah pulled his attention back to the phone. "What were they doing, when you caught them?"

She was quiet for a moment before answering.

"Are you alone?" she asked.

"You should know," he said.

"Oh, don't take it so hard," she said. "I'm only here because you screwed up Ghana and Eli doesn't trust you anymore."

Jonah let that one slide. Eli sent Keeler. Keeler was a variable — one Jonah warned Eli about. *Eli* screwed up Ghana.

"Where are you right now?" he said.

"Admiring the flowers."

"Where," he repeated.

"Storage room," she said. "Subfloor."

"Don't move," he said, and he hung up the phone.

52

GAVIN

GAVIN WAS RUNNING, BENT DOUBLE. HIS BACKPACK, sliding forward, was falling around his neck as he tried to stay low and keep from being seen. He stopped at another cover, to rest. It was a large terracotta potted plant. The image of the woman with the gun was frozen in his mind. This, he thought, was definitely *not* the Botanical Gardens security they were dealing with. He'd pulled out his phone again. His hands were shaking as he found Erin's number in the recent calls list. He pushed the button and put the phone to his ear. He could barely hear the phone ringing over his own heart pounding.

"Erin—" he started and then immediately caught himself. He swore out loud. It was an automated message. Again. This was the second time he'd tried her. *Why wasn't she picking up?*

The plan had been for Gavin to cover the expected meeting areas with hidden cameras. That would be the evidence they'd need for Erin and Eli Bren's meeting. And so far, he had exactly two cameras in place. Nowhere near enough. And now, he was having a hard time concentrating. It was taking everything he could muster just to not lose it. He dropped the phone down by his side.

"Think," he said to himself. "*Think.*"

He knew Jonah Lennox was setting up this meeting. And that he would be here tonight. But he didn't know when that was happening. Or, not to mention — if they could even trust Lennox. He remembered him from Ghana. And despite what *Erin* believed about Lennox, Gavin wasn't convinced. Not even close. He'd seen him first hand. He knew what he was capable of. Jonah Lennox was *not* a good man. And now Gavin was wondering if this was all his doing. Another double-cross.

He had to get in touch with Erin.

He fingered his phone again. His sweaty hands kept slipping off the buttons as he tried to dial. He put it to his ear. It was ringing. And ringing. And then… nothing. He closed his eyes, leaning his head back against the big pot. His options were running out. And if he didn't warn Erin, she'd be walking into this blind. And it was looking a lot like a trap. Not to mention, that woman, she took Ben and Hale at gunpoint. His mind was racing.

But, despite every fear threatening to overtake him right now… he was beginning to develop another plan. Well, not a plan. More of a next step. And it was scaring him more than anything else.

He opened his eyes and stood up. Straightening the pack on his back, he looked around. Erin wasn't answering her phone. Nothing he could do about that. And setting up the rest of the cameras — that would have to wait.

He knew what he needed to do right now. Ben and Hale needed him now. He started walking. He didn't see where the woman had taken them. And, without a gun — though, his situation he wouldn't be much different *with* a gun — he didn't have much of a chance of helping them when he did find them. But he had to try. He had to do *something*.

53

LOST

Erin let the phone drop next to her.

She'd just opened her motel door, getting back after the narrow miss at the convenience store. She hadn't even shut the door yet when her phone rang.

It was Jonah. He was brief.

Val had taken Hale.

And Ben.

He told her not to think about them. To stick with the plan.

She knew what that meant. Jonah wasn't the type to beat around the bush. But he was putting it to her like this — softening the blow, if such a thing was possible — so that she didn't quit. So that she continued on.

But what he wasn't telling her, what he didn't have to tell her, was that if Val had them, then it would only be a matter of time, if it hadn't happened already, before she— Erin couldn't bring herself to go there. Even as she knew it to be true.

Vaguely, she could hear Jonah, still talking. The burner flip-phone was on the floor, still open, laying on its side.

Erin's hand moved itself to cover her mouth. She slid down inside the frame of the door. The night's bitter cold wind was flipping through her hair. But she didn't feel any of it.

She's been playing the odds. And, until now, she had a good hand. But… then… then the house laid down its hand.

And it was better.

The house had beat her.

Every gambler knows, if you play long enough, the house wins. It's always that way. Because the house can take hit after hit after hit, reaching into its deep pockets, to still survive.

It's the gambler who can't.

She didn't mean to, but she started crying. She realized now how much her plan had been a gamble. All of it. Bringing in Gavin and Hale. Letting Ben go. And now — her heart was beginning to stop, to freeze up — because, now they were all gone.

Forever.

Whatever future she and Ben had— she choked at the thought of it.

There was just… nothing.

And Paul.

What would he think… He gave his life for all of this. And then he gave *her* the keys to finish the work. But there was nothing left to finish. She'd lost it all.

She fell over on her side, sobbing. She couldn't help it. Her body wasn't hers anymore. She was convulsing, not in pain, or fear, or even guilt — but in loss.

She'd let everyone around her be thrown to the lions. And the lions were so hungry. She would throw herself next. What else was there… If Eli Bren had made this move, then he was never going to go along with her. Her plan, her ideas, her belief that maybe she could get through to him — it had all been so stupid. Naive. Just like… just like Jonah had told her in the diner.

There had been so much loss. For so many years. And she just wanted to fix it.

But now, all she'd done was make it worse.

She hadn't fixed anything at all.

She'd just caused more people to be lost.

The truth about her mother, all of Paul's work, and everyone else — everything was lost.

She looked up, still sitting in the frame of the open door of her motel room. The inside, her room, was dark. She hadn't even turned on the lights. And the outside, it was dark, too. Up above her, as she looked, not quite able to focus, she thought she could see stars. Or… maybe it was just her own consciousness slipping away.

Whatever.

She didn't care anymore. Any path now that was willing to take her, was fine. As long as it carried her, doing the work for her, she'd let it.

For now, and forever, that would be enough.

54

NEW

Erin pulled herself off the floor. The motel door was still open. She used the frame to support her weight as she stood. She wasn't sure if she'd passed out or not. But she could feel the cold now. On her hands and on her face. She took a step inside her room and shut the door behind her. The inside was still and frozen and dark. She flipped on the light and walked to the mirror over the dresser.

She looked at herself.

She was tired.

And sorry.

But more than that, she was angry. Angry enough to be reckless. But… not like she's been before. Not unaware of the consequences. Or the people that might get hurt in the process. No, this was different. The recklessness she now felt surging through her veins was all about her. Standing there now, she had a complete lack of self-preservation. Whatever it took, she'd do it.

What had changed, she wondered… She looked down at her watch — her train of thought shifted. She'd been on the floor longer than she realized. And she had to go. *Now.*

She looked at herself once more. Like an old friend she hadn't seen in a long while… and probably wouldn't see again for quite a bit longer, if ever. She reached into her bag and grabbed a few twenties and the pistol Jonah had given her at the diner. She balled the first up and pushed them down into her front pocket, the one that still held the recorder from before. And she slid the second into the small of her back, pulling her jacket down to cover it.

She turned away from the mirror without looking again and walked toward the door. She reached down and picked up her burner phone on the way out, leaving everything else behind.

Outside she called for a cab. She started walking. The night was cold. But it didn't bother her anymore. As she kept walking, she started to wish the cold *would* bother her more. That it would feel… *cold*, like it did before. There was something normalizing about that kind of discomfort. But that was gone. Whatever switch had flipped inside of her, whatever it was that had steeled her resolve to go into this — to die — it seemed to have desensitized her.

But no, that wasn't right. She wasn't *less* focused than before. Her mind was sharp. More than before. And, as she walked, she could feel it. It was as if, for the first time, she had *only* focus. None of the other fears or thoughts mattered. She knew what she needed to do. And… she would do it.

The cab was up ahead at the corner, waiting.

She opened the door and got in.

"U.S. Botanical Gardens," she told the driver.

The guy eyed her through his rearview mirror. "You know it's closed this time of night, right?"

"Yes," she said.

"Alright then," he said. He put his blinker on and pulled out onto the street.

As the car moved through the night, it was quiet. The

entire city was peaceful, at home, with family. It was ironic, that she too, would be spending her night with family. Though, there would be nothing peaceful about it. And, just as tonight would be her first in some ways, it would probably be her last in just about every other way.

55

CONSERVATORY

The cab stopped on Independence Ave, at the front of the Conservatory. It had a sweeping glass dome ceiling, built up high in the middle with glass all along the sides, making it appear from the street that the entire roof was glass. Being in the U.S. Mall, near the Capitol, the place was well lit.

The driver stopped out front. She passed him a few twenties, not waiting for change.

She stepped out of the cab. As she did, the driver rolled down his window behind her.

"You going to be okay?"

"Yes," she said without turning around. She could hear the cab's tires pulling away. She pulled out her phone and dialed Jonah's number. He answered on the first ring.

"I'm here," she said.

"South entrance," he told her. The phone went dead.

She began walking. A moment later, she was around the back. The entire property was made for walking. She reached out a hand, to pull open one of the doors. Normally, after closing, these would be locked. This one opened before she could put her hand on it.

It was Jonah. He was standing in the doorway.

He didn't look around, to see if she was alone, or if anyone else might see them. He just looked at her. She walked in, and he let the door shut behind her.

Without saying anything, he started walking into the interior. She followed him.

"Where are they," she said to his back. She was talking about Ben and Hale.

He didn't answer her.

"Are they—" but her voice cracked. She swallowed. "Are they still alive?" she said, pushing the words out.

He continued to walk. "Probably," he said, without turning around.

"Probably?" she said, her voice rising. At this point, she didn't care who heard her. She reached out and grabbed his shoulder, to make him stop walking and look at her. He did stop and he turned around, facing her.

"First things first," he said. His voice was cold. Like he'd done this sort of thing a hundred times before. "They'll be using them as leverage. Against you. Going after them first is a mistake. They'll expect that. If you can't let them go, you can't win this."

Erin understood. Better than she wanted to.

"*Are* they still alive?" she asked again.

"Hale will take some time to recover."

"And?"

"And so far they haven't touched Ben."

"That's… good news, at least," Erin said.

"No," Jonah said. "It's not. It means they've done their homework. Hale was a free sample. They hurt him so that you'll visual what they'll do next. And then, at any point you don't do exactly what they want, then they'll do it to Ben, in front of you this time. Until you do what they want, how they want."

Erin hadn't anticipated this. She knew from his call earlier, that they'd captured Ben and Hale. And that… that they might kill them. But she'd looked at that as an isolated series of events. Collateral to the rest. Not a factor still in play — a lever now used to manipulate her.

"Then…," she said, looking up at him. "What do we do?"

"We do exactly what we planned."

"But—" she started, shaking her head.

"No," he said. He was quieter now. "We do exactly what we planned."

He stopped talking, still looking at her.

"Clear?"

She nodded. What else was there? He turned around and started walking again. She closed her eyes and opened them, and then walked after him.

56

ELI

stretch of a large open area. He was alone. And lit by the
always-on lights above. They cast shadows on his face. Maybe
it was the angle of the lights. Or maybe she was seeing him
perfectly clear now. But his face looked dark. Like the devil.

Jonah walked forward, stopped and turned to her.

"Stop," he said to her.

She stopped walking.

"Hold up your hands."

He began to frisk her. But he didn't try hard. Eli was a
good forty feet away from them. Jonah felt the contents of
her pants pockets from the outside. He reached into her
jacket, moving his hands quickly around her torso. He
reached down into the middle of her lower back and pulled
out the gun.

She looked at him. She wanted to say *no*. That he could
just lie and say she didn't have anything. His eyes met hers.
But they weren't smug, as they usually were. They were serious. As he took the gun from her, it was as if, with his eyes,
he was… giving it back to her. She didn't understand. He

held the gun out to the side, for Eli to see, still facing her. Still not breaking eye contact with Erin. His face was completely still. She saw years and years in his face. Far beyond her own. Though, she knew he was, at best, just a decade older than her. He looked so much older right now.

He turned and called out to Eli. "That's it." He tossed the gun forward, off to the side. Erin's eyes were trained on Eli now, but, through her peripheral vision, she only saw where the gun landed. In some bushes, nearby, in between them and Eli.

"Well," Eli called out, "do come in. I believe we have… *things* to discuss."

She walked forward, not saying anything. Jonah walked forward, but let Erin take the lead. He moved off to the side.

Eli spoke again. "You know, I was beginning to think you weren't going to come."

Erin still didn't respond.

"Look," he said, his tone was almost congenial. "I hope you're still not upset about Paul."

Erin knew what Eli was trying to do. It was a power play. It wasn't enough to hold all the cards. He wanted to make sure she understood at every step of the way: *He* was in charge.

Eli was still talking.

"Paul was… *not* a reasonable man," Eli said. "And he," Eli lifted his hands, as if he were searching for a respectful way to put it: "Well, he was going to get himself killed eventually. It was really just unfortunate timing that it happened there, as it did."

Erin still didn't respond. She was standing about twenty feet from him now. She stopped walking.

"Anyway," Eli said, looking down at the watch on his wrist. "I've got a lot to do. Let's get on with this."

Erin spoke finally. Her heart was pounding through her

chest. And until she heard the words come out of her mouth, she wasn't sure she'd actually be able *to* talk.

"Do," she said. "Do you know who I am?" There were so many plants filling up the cavernous room, that, even without all the people that would normally be there when the place was open, there was still no echo. It's as if, once her voice left her mouth, it completely disappeared.

"Of course," Eli said. His voice boomed into the space. A stark comparison to her own.

"And did you know who my mother was?" Erin said.

This, strictly speaking, wasn't part of Erin's plan. But now that she was here, she couldn't help herself. Eli's gaze faltered. Was it shame? she wondered. She kept watching him. No, not shame. It was something else. Something dark. Hate.

"I do," he said, quietly, with venom.

"And is that why you agreed to meet me tonight?"

"In a manner of speaking," he said.

She let his words linger. It was her turn to talk. She'd taken the lead in this exchange. And she knew she needed to say something. But she'd expected him to offer more. To explain. To justify. Not just acknowledge…

"Why," she said. It wasn't a question. And, inside, she already knew the answer. But, if nothing else went right tonight, he would account for himself. At the very least, she wanted to hear him say the words.

"Why," she said again, louder.

Eli shook his head. "No," he said quietly.

"No?" Erin said.

But Eli had turned. He wasn't looking at her anymore. He was looking off to his side.

"Val," he called out. "If you would."

Val walked out from the side, not far from where Eli was.

Erin's face flushed. She felt pure rage seeing her. It had been Eli in charge that day in Colombia. But it had been *Val* who pulled the trigger, who killed Paul. And when she did it, when Paul fell, she still remembered Val's face. Frozen forever in her mind's eye. She couldn't forget. And in that image she held onto, she remembered clearly seeing a look of satisfaction in Val's eyes. As if she'd just done a good thing, killing Paul. And as Val walked out now, she saw the same expression.

But she wasn't alone.

Beside her walked a duct-taped Hale.

And Ben.

"Now," Eli said, looking at Erin again. "You're going to answer all of *my* questions."

Erin was looking at Ben. He was, as Jonah said, unharmed. And, remembering what *else* Jonah said, about him being used as a tool, in front of her, it was making her sick. Knowing what would be happening to him next… and that it was all because of her.

She glanced down, away from Ben. And then back at Eli. She nodded her head.

Yes.

She was ready.

57

GAVIN

Gavin could see everything. He went looking for Ben and Hale earlier. And he found them. But they were locked up, tight. That woman, the one who was now holding them, had been keeping a close eye on them. He looked at her, closely, and he realized, something about her reminded him of Erin. And then it hit him, *she* must have been the same one that killed the senator. It all fit. And, from a distance, if the two were wearing the same clothes, he imagined it wouldn't be hard to confuse them.

He pulled back. Unless something happened, unless something here changed, he was stuck and there was nothing he could do. Nothing he could do, that is, that wouldn't be offering himself up. And then he'd certainly be no help. He looked down at his throwaway phone. He flipped it open. The battery light was on. He swore under his breath. He tried calling Erin again. But where they were, in that area underneath the Conservatory, there was no signal. He looked at his phone again as the battery light faded. The thing had died. "No," he swore to himself again.

He shoved it back in his pocket and continued to watch.

Mostly, he was focusing on not losing control. He'd been fighting a massive panic attack since this started. And then, when that seemed to be waning, he noticed a new problem — he could not move. It was as if the rest of his body had stopped responding to the commands from his brain.

He'd always liked adventure. But more in an academic way. When he worked with Paul, he was living out in the bush. But it was never a fight to survive. Not literally. They were often out in the middle of nowhere. But they'd portaled in some of the nice things of modern life, too. Like internet. And toilets. But in all of that time, the only *real* threat he'd come across was when he ran out of malaria medicine and got sick.

But now, this was different.

And… he wasn't handling it well. He wanted to move, to finish setting up the cameras. But he couldn't bring himself to do it. To risk it.

A few times, he saw the woman talking to someone else. Once Jonah came down and talked to her face to face. He wanted to follow after him. To talk to him. And tell him he was there, too. But Jonah seemed pretty comfortable with this woman. And, it was what Gavin had thought from the beginning. Jonah wasn't on their side. Not really. He was just playing them.

Then, that's when they all started to move.

Val took Ben and Hale and walked them out, up the stairs into the main area. Gavin had followed from a distance. And upstairs, on the main floor, he could see Erin. She was here. And someone else was too. An older man. He figured that was Eli Bren. Watching the older man, a chill went up the back of Gavin's neck. He looked again at Erin. There had to be something he could do. But *what*… He continued to watch. And wait…

58

WATCHING

ELI ASKED ERIN A FEW QUESTIONS, WHICH SHE answered. And then, it was almost as if he had slipped into a new mode. As if he was reflecting on his life. It was strange to listen to.

"My children," he said, looking at Jonah as he said the words, "have largely been… a disappointment."

Erin wanted to look over at Jonah, to see his reaction. But she didn't. She kept her eyes trained on Eli. Erin slowly began to take off her jacket. Not making any sudden moves. It *was* hot in the room. But she wasn't feeling the temperature. She held her jacket for a moment in front of her, before tossing it aside. Eli was still talking. About life, and family, and a bunch of other things.

"Val," he said — and smiled as he looked in her direction, "has become a bit like a daughter over the years." He said more. Some things he talked about Erin didn't understand. He made references that, she assumed, was more for Jonah's sake than for hers.

As she stood there, with Jonah off to the side, she had the

strangest feeling. The closest she'd ever had to having a family was before her mother died. She was only eight when that happened. And before then, her mother had traveled a good bit of time, too. After that, it was her aunt who raised her. But it was never the same. Family had always been something other people had.

But now, standing here — her father was in front of her, and her brother, or half-brother, was there, too. For all of her life, she wanted something like this. But this, this was nothing like she wanted. And now, at this moment, what she really wanted was for it all to just end.

Eli was still talking, but Erin interrupted him.

"Why are you doing this?" she said.

He paused.

"…telling me all of this…," she added.

It's as if he were genuinely thinking about the question.

"I suppose," he said. "It's just the ramblings of an old man."

But before Erin could respond, Eli said something else.

Just one word.

"Val."

She lifted her gun. For a tight painful second, Erin thought she was going to shoot *Ben*.

But she didn't. She held it, trained forward, past Ben. To her.

Val pulled the trigger and the end exploded.

But the bullet didn't hit Erin.

The crack of gunfire was so loud she thought it would set off alarms or break the glass or something. Erin had involuntarily closed her eyes. But when she reopened them, Val was still there, still holding the gun. But it… *wasn't* pointed at Erin at all. Slightly away. Erin followed its trajectory, from the tip in Val's hand, to where the bullet had gone. To Jonah. Lying on the ground.

"Jonah," Erin called out.

She started to run to him.

But a booming voice stopped her. Eli the 'old man' was once again Eli 'the devil.'

"Stop," he called out.

And she did. Something about his voice made it almost impossible to resist. But she was still watching Jonah. He pulled himself up onto his elbows. He was off to the side, near the bushes. And he held his hands up, examining them as he put his weight on his elbows. His hands were slick with blood.

"Well that was cheap," he said. But his voice was low. Despite the levity of his reply, Erin could tell the bullet had done a lot of damage.

She wanted to go to him. To help him. And she started again, to move. But she heard Eli speak again, and she again stopped.

"I wouldn't," Eli said.

Erin turned to look back toward Eli and Val. And now, Val's gun was trained on her.

She froze, knowing clearly what was coming next.

Off to the side, Jonah was beginning to stand up.

Eli said something else. But his words were too soft for Erin to hear. And then, Val took a step back. She walked to where Ben was standing. She stepped behind him, wrapping an arm around his middle, almost as if she were hugging him from behind. Something Erin might have done. Ben's mouth was covered with tape. But Erin could see his breathing pick up. Val looked around him, so that Erin could see her face. And then, she lifted her other hand, the one holding the gun, and let its tip touch Ben's temple.

A smile, the same satisfied smile that was burned into Erin's memory from the last time she'd seen Val. When she'd killed Paul.

She called out to Erin. The first thing Erin had heard her say tonight. Still with her smile. "Are you watching?"

59

RUNNING

Gavin was moving now. He wasn't setting up cameras. There was no time. He saw the woman, standing behind Ben and putting her gun to his head. And after what she'd done to Hale, and probably others, Gavin wasn't doubting her. He didn't think she was bluffing.

Gavin saw something on the other side. A Christmas exhibit. And it had a tall centerpiece. Part of it loomed over where Erin and the others were. And a new idea was taking shape. It was thin. But it was the last hour now. If he could somehow get to it…

He started moving. He was almost running now, doubled over, so that no one could see him.

He stopped moving, taking cover and looking up again. Partially, he wanted to make sure no one had spotted him. But mostly, he needed to see what had changed. Was she still pointing the gun at Ben? As he scanned the scene below, he saw it. And then he heard it… The click. The woman pulling back the hammer on the gun. It didn't echo. But the sound pierced the room nonetheless.

Gavin got up again, and he was running flat out now. Or,

as 'flat out' as he could while still trying not to be seen. He'd almost tripped twice. He was going the long way, to make it around without being seen. It was still faster this way, because, now that he was out of line of sight from the scene below, he could run properly. As he ran, a stitch was beginning to pull at his side. He kept pushing forward. Willing himself to move. Not giving in to the growing pain. He started making a promise to himself. If he got out of this, he'd exercise every single day of life. He was slowing down, and breathing harder, but he was almost there.

60

CRASHING DOWN

Erin noticed something catch Val's attention. Something behind where Erin was standing. But Val's focus soon returned to the situation at hand. Erin knew she needed to do something. To stop the inevitable. Val was still holding the gun on Ben. And he was tied. As it was… he couldn't help. If he moved to escape, or do anything, she'd immediately shoot him. Erin knew that about Val. She wasn't trigger-shy.

But then, Erin didn't have to do anything. Not yet. Because Eli started speaking. As he did, Val relaxed, taking her cue from him for the moment. She was still holding the gun on Ben. Nothing had changed. But, at least, they had a few more minutes…

Eli was talking now. "I think all parents," he said, "feel a swell of pride when their children follow in their footsteps. You" — he was looking at Erin — "never did. Your mother, as soon as she figured out that some of my ventures didn't meet her approval, was bent on stopping me. She never understood the greater good. It was always black and white, right and wrong, with her. But the world isn't built like that."

Eli was talking like he had no hurry or no other concern. Like this was just a normal conversation, and like now was a normal time to have it. As he talked, Erin kept watching Val, with her gun still on Ben. Hale was sitting behind the rest. He was tied. And Erin could see how badly he'd been beaten up. She could tell he was breathing, but he may have lost consciousness. He wasn't moving.

Eli was still talking. "I knew Gillian had a daughter," he said. "And I knew it was you. I wondered if you'd be like her. Strong. That was the thing about Gillian," he said, as if remembering something fondly. "She *was* strong." Erin thought it was strange the way he was telling her these things. Almost as if he'd never truly been able to tell anyone else these things before, and then, now, here, he finally could.

He looked at Erin, talking directly to her now. "I tested you, you know."

"Tested me?" Erin said.

"To see if you were like her. To see if you were like me… A few years ago. You'd graduated from school, and, like your mother, you couldn't leave well enough alone. You were working on the case she'd been working on when she died."

"When you killed her," Erin corrected him.

He kept talking, like he didn't notice her words. "You didn't know I was involved then. When you went down to Trinidad. But you did better than I thought. And you were getting too close."

A chill went through Erin's body. She opened her mouth to speak. But it was a moment before her body caught up and the words came out.

"What…," she started, the words getting caught on their way out. "What are you saying?"

"I sent someone. To Trinidad. To stop you."

"You?"

"I wanted to see how you'd react," he said. "If you would

die for your principles, like your mother. Or if you were a survivor, and a conqueror, like me."

Erin's mind was racing to catch up. He was talking about orchestrating what happened in Trinidad all those years ago. She'd learned a lot recently from Paul's files. But he didn't have anything about this. Paul was there. He was the one who'd saved her. She knew that from his notes. But when it came to who was behind it, that was apparently a mystery to Paul, too. Or, if he knew, it didn't show up anywhere in his notes. At least, not that Erin found.

"You're saying," Erin started, her voice was quiet. "That you sent the men, in Trinidad, to kidnap me…"

"I needed to know what you were made of. But apparently I wasn't the only one who was keeping an eye on you. Paul Dannon," Eli's face changed as he said the name. "Dannon stepped in and made a mess of things."

"No," Erin said. "Paul stepped in and *saved* me. From you."

Eli seemed to find this, the last part Erin said, amusing. He didn't laugh. It was as if he was thinking about something else as she said these words. And then, a new thought came into Erin's mind. A small thought. One that had been gnawing at her for some time. But until now, it had been too small — compared to everything else — for her to properly consider it. But… there was something about what Eli was saying right now. Something about his body language that caused this new idea to pop into her head. Ghana, she thought. The golden chair…

Erin pushed the words out. "Ghana," she said. "Why."

Eli didn't immediately answer. He shook his head slowly, and looked to Jonah before looking back again at Erin.

Eli let out a low breath. "My father…," he said. "He was not a good man. But he did good work. And he passed on to me an important love of history." His face changed a little as he was saying the words. "Some cultures," Eli said, "if left to themselves, they destroy themselves. Ultimately, as history has shown us, they are weak. Not meant to survive. The chair, it was an important — if not largely forgotten — part of history. Not because of the people who owned it. They were the weak ones. The ones destined to die. The chair was important because it was a lesson. Of this very thing. And so I sent Jonah…," he paused, "to bring it back."

Erin glanced over at Jonah. He was standing now. But he'd lost a lot of blood. His face was pale. Most of his torso was covered in blood. Given the way he was standing, or struggling to, Erin figured Val hit him in the thigh, missing any vitals. But Erin could tell he was still bleeding, and he wouldn't last too much longer like this.

Eli continued. But he was talking about Carl and R4 now, where, not too long ago, she used to work. Erin knew Eli was on the board. She'd met him a few times, though only briefly. And it was Carl who was recently arrested for attempting to kill Erin in everything that went down in Ghana. Not directly, he was technically booked for hiring someone else to do the job. But… his involvement had been a mystery to Erin. What had he been caught up in, that pushed him into that? Into betraying her and trying to have her killed… But, it was only now, as Eli was talking, that she began to understand how it all connected. It wasn't *Carl*. Not really. He was just Eli's pawn. Like so many others…

"We acquired R4 after Carl Ibsen failed to keep it afloat," Eli said. "Ibsen was shrewd, but, ultimately, he was weak. After Trinidad, I'd been keeping an eye on you. You'd dropped the case. But a source told me you hadn't *really* dropped it. And so I knew I'd need to remove you. For good."

"Like my mother," Erin said.

She was angry now as she listened to him talk about her,

like he was some puppet master. And she was angry for how much he really *had* orchestrated. Angry too… that she hadn't put it together before now…

"Recently," he said. "I saw the opportunity to kill two birds with one stone. We could grab the artifact from Ghana and preserve it, something the Ghanaians could never do. And I would tie up *this* loose end," he nodded to Erin as he said the last words.

It was surreal, hearing him talk so cavalierly about her. Like he showed no shame. And…apparently, he didn't.

"So I had Ibsen, your boss, send you to Ghana. It should have been as simple as that." He looked again to Jonah as he said it. "But I underestimated a certain level of… incompetence." He turned fully to look at Jonah. "I had more hope for you. After all those years…"

Erin could hear Jonah moving again. She looked at him, and saw him, still standing, he'd lifted his head and was looking at Eli. His body was fading. But he wasn't defeated. Erin could see that. Jonah spoke.

"Lillian," he said. His voice was raspy now, but it wasn't weak.

"Lillian," Eli repeated, almost with a laugh. But it wasn't a laugh. There was too much disgust in his voice for that. "You betrayed me… for *her*?"

Jonah kept his eyes on Eli, not blinking.

"She had cancer," Eli said. "She was already dying. There was nothing that could be done."

Jonah started to move. He kept his eyes on Eli as he did. But he wasn't walking toward Eli, he was moving toward Erin.

"Son," Eli said. "Her death was the best thing that could have happened to you. You were a weak child with her still alive." Eli was almost spitting as he talked. "And she… she was a weak woman. You would have been worthless if she'd raised you. *That's* why I stepped in. To make you into something."

Eli stopped talking. He was breathing heavily, as if he'd just walked up a set of stairs. He glanced at Val, and she pulled the gun away from Ben's head. But she didn't put it down by her side. She lifted it toward Jonah, and Erin.

This new scene Erin was looking at, the one where Eli held all the cards, was beginning to come into sharper focus now. She understood why Eli had agreed to meet her tonight. It wasn't because of her. He didn't *need* anything from her. He must have believed Jonah was already working against him. He must have wanted to see it play out. And then handle it all at one time…

Val's gun held Erin and Jonah still as Eli began talking again. Slower this time…

"The fugitive Erin Reed, who killed the patriot, Senator Avery Cleason, was meeting her accomplice Jonah Lennox when a dispute broke out. She shot him. Or he shot her. We're not sure who started it. But a lot of gunfire was exchanged. And, in the end, both died."

Eli stopped for effect.

"How does that sound for a story?" he said. "And don't worry, it'll hold up. We've already planted the evidence."

Ben moved, but just slightly. His movement caught her eye. And she looked at him. As she did, she could feel a tear moving down her face.

"Do it," Eli said to Val, his face twisted in an ugly, violent rage.

"Wait," someone said. Erin thought it was Ben. But his mouth was still taped. No, it was Jonah, behind her. "You're missing something, Eli."

Eli held up a hand for Val to wait.

"It's always the same. You rush forward, and you fall," Jonah said. Erin could hear his voice failing him as he said the words. "Even before you know it, you've fallen. You think about your strengths and forget about your weaknesses."

Jonah stopped talking. Erin could hear him breathing. She didn't know if he's stopped to make a point. Or if he's stopped because he was having trouble going on.

"Enough of this," Eli said. "Kill them both."

Val took aim. But the next sounds that came weren't from her gun. It was a terrible, tearing sound. A cacophony of noise coming from off to the left. A large botanical Christmas display was crashing down in the middle of where Erin, Eli and the rest were standing. Erin and Jonah had to move to keep it from hitting them.

As Erin looked in the direction of the chaos, someone was there, off to the side. Someone waving and calling her name.

It was Gavin.

61

DEAD

THE NEXT SOUND ERIN HEARD WAS GUNFIRE. SHE looked up to see Val walking toward them, her gun in her hand, extended, and firing at her and Jonah.

Jonah got up, with more speed than Erin though him capable of at this point. But he didn't run toward Val. Or even away, for cover. He moved to where Erin was. In front of her. She thought for a moment, he was trying to say something to her. Or, that maybe he was confused — thinking she had cover, when she didn't. She was just as exposed as he.

She wanted to move — to run. But he grabbed on to her, keeping her there. He pulled her down. If they stayed here, they would be dead. They *needed* to move. But at the same time, Erin knew she had nowhere else to go. Val was on them. And there was no cover they could get to in time. Especially not Jonah, with all the blood he'd lost. And even if Erin did find somewhere to hide, Ben or Hale, and maybe even Gavin, they would all be tools for Val to use, hostages to bring Erin back.

Jonah was almost smothering Erin now, laying on top of her. In his raspy voice, he was yelling something. Or trying to. With the gunfire and everything else, Erin was having a hard time making out the words. It sounded like he was saying "take it." But Erin didn't know what that meant.

And then, something else happened.

Jonah's body shook a few times. Erin could feel it, as he laid on top of her. And then, he stopped moving. Stopped holding her down. His muscles that were so tense a second before, were limp now. She felt the warmth, too. The blood from the bullet holes, seeping out of his body, and onto hers.

Then, she understood. He'd been covering her. Using himself as a shield. To save her. *Jonah* saved her. She closed her eyes tight. She didn't know what else to do. And she just laid there, hoping the end would come soon.

But Erin could tell, Jonah wasn't moving anymore. She lightly called his name. Something just he'd hear. But nothing came in response. No words and no motion.

And then, with that, she realized…

Jonah was dead.

● 62

DOUBLED BACK

Erin's face was still mostly buried under one of Jonah's arms. The rest of her body was pinned under his weight.

But she kept hearing him. Not him — but the words he'd told her, just before… just before he'd gone. He'd said, "take it." She was sure of it now. And then, she began to understand. Without opening her eyes, or getting up, she began to move her free hand. It was under his body, but it wasn't pinned.

She moved carefully, trying not to draw any extra attention. To preserve whatever edge she might still have. She knew what she had to do now.

She could also feel someone coming closer. And as she listened, she could hear other sounds. At first, she thought it might be Ben. Or maybe Gavin. She prayed they were still alive.

And then, from under Jonah, she could see a shadow, appearing next to her. She opened her eyes, still covered by Jonah's arm. And she could see men's dress shoes. Eli Bren. She heard him talking.

"Fix this," he said. "Arrange it like we discussed." He must be talking to Val.

Erin had stopped moving. She had no idea what she looked like, from their vantage point, with Jonah on top of her. But they apparently didn't realize she wasn't dead yet. And she didn't want to lose that edge. No matter how small it was. Eli's shoes moved away, and Erin slowly started moving her hand again. Feeling around. Being quick and careful.

She heard Eli saying a few other things.

The tone of his voice… so clinical and cold.

And what he'd done, as she laid there, it was sinking in. He'd just killed his *son*. One who'd been with him all these years. And, not to forget, he'd *meant* to kill his daughter, too. Her. Erin. Just like he'd killed her mother, Gillian. And Paul. And so many others.

With this, Erin felt a surge of power come through her. It was a lot like shock in that it didn't feel like her. It felt like she was living through someone else. But, in another way, it was the exact opposite of shock. There was not a single bit of numbness in her right now. She was *completely* connected. Everything inside her had been turned up to eleven.

Her heart-rate.

Her mind, now calculating.

He strength, preparing her to move.

Her sense of touch, feeling everything.

And, even her hearing.

She heard more footsteps, but they were softer. Not Eli's. Val's.

Erin kept moving her hand, under Jonah's body.

And then, without warning, Jonah stood up, getting off of her.

But his body was as limp as ever. His head hung as Val moved his body. And then, when she pulled him off, Erin saw for the first time, what Val had done. There was so much blood. His entire front was covered in red. She already knew he was gone. But seeing him like this… He was completely wrecked. It put in her a fresher sense of fear and pain, and — more than anything else — hate.

As Val pulled his body off, the gun Jonah was holding shifted and fell, into Erin's hand. It was what Jonah had been trying to give her before. And she understood now. "Take it" was the gun. He'd pulled it off of her earlier, so that Eli and Val wouldn't. So that he could give it back to her. And, when he died — when he put himself in front of her, taking Val's bullets — that's what he was doing.

Erin pulled herself up, onto her knees, holding out the gun. She raised, seeing only Jonah, but knowing Val was behind him, carrying him.

Erin pulling back on the trigger, hard.

The gun rocked over and over in her hands. Jonah's body fell. And with it, Val's. Now he was pinning her.

Erin stood and ran to them, the gun still out in front of her. Both of her elbows were locked.

She'd hit Val. But she wasn't done.

Erin stood over her. Not daring to take her eyes off of her. Or to even blink.

Images from Colombia were flooding her mind. Of Paul, crouched down, with his rifle, on the top floor of Eli Bren's tower. And of Val gunning him down.

Standing over Val now, Erin pulled the trigger.

Again.

And again.

And again.

The gun kept rocking up and down with every explosion. Even at point-blank, she wasn't sure she was hitting her. But Val wasn't moving.

Erin stopped shooting. She wasn't sure why exactly. She

wasn't *ready* to stop. She wanted to keep going. To keep shooting Val. To kill her a thousand more times.

Everything was still now, except for Erin's chest. Rising and falling, as she caught her breath. She kept her eyes on Val. Her body was empty. The bullets had made a mess of her. And there was no doubt to Erin. Val was dead.

Erin took a step back, letting the gun, still in her hand, point down to the floor.

But then, there was a new sound, off to the side. Erin snapped to it. Shifting her weight and her body, raising the gun and pointing it in the direction of the new sound.

It was Eli.

He was standing there, watching it all.

For a moment, no one said anything. Erin stood with her gun pointed at him. Eli stood, watching her. And then, finally, he spoke.

"Come with me," he said.

She heard the words in her mind. She knew what they meant. But she didn't consider them. Not even for a second. That way, with him, was only death. And she'd had enough death…

She lowered her gun, just an inch. And took a step toward him. She didn't know why, or what she was going to do next. Still, something outside of herself was moving her.

"We could—" Eli started.

But she interrupted him.

"Stop," she yelled. She couldn't stand to hear another word. Nothing else from him. And then… at that moment, she knew something else was true. That she had to stop this. Forever. Now. And she had to do it.

The gun was still in her hands, pointed out. She lifted it back up, putting it level with his head.

"Erin," he said. She could see his lips move. Hear the sound hit her ears. But all she was doing was steadying her breath. She inhaled, long and smooth. And with that, before exhaling, steady as she could, she pulled the trigger once more.

But nothing happened this time.

The gun clicked…but it didn't shake. She pulled on it again. Nothing.

She'd emptied the gun on Val moments ago.

"I guess," Eli said, taking a step back. "That's it then."

He kept walking backward as he said it, not taking his eyes off of her. Neither did Erin drop the gun. Even though it was empty. Holding it still gave her power. And it seemed like both she and Eli understood that. He moved back into a shadow, until she couldn't see him anymore. And she heard his footsteps move faster. He was gone.

She dropped down to her knees. The empty metal gun clanking as it hit the ground. She crawled to where Jonah was. She wanted to see Jonah as much as she didn't want to see him. Not like this. But she couldn't help it. She pulled his body off of Val's. Not wanting him to be anywhere near her. Val's own gun, still in her hand, slipped out. It was dark. Quite a bit larger than the one Jonah had given Erin.

And then, she thought of Ben. She turned her head. A new surge of energy picked her up. And as she stood, she saw Ben. He was already there.

But it wasn't right.

Something was… off.

Ben was still tied. Still taped. And not walking toward her. Just standing there.

And then Erin saw… Ben wasn't alone.

Eli hadn't left after all.

He was back.

And he had a gun this time — on Ben.

PART TWO

"MY GUN HAS BULLETS, AND YOURS DOESN'T," ELI SAID. "It's as simple as that. Now, back up and lie on the ground."

Eli had one hand on Ben. His other was holding a gun, pressed into Ben's temple.

Erin stayed still, not moving. She kept her eyes pinned to Eli.

"Do it," he said.

He took the gun away from Ben's head and pointed it now at Erin. The two were only about twenty feet apart. He could easily hit her from here. And, she knew, there was nowhere to go. But still… she didn't move. It wasn't that she couldn't. It was just that she… didn't.

"No," she said.

As the sound came out of her mouth, her eyes darted down to Val's large dark gun on the floor next to her dead body. It wasn't far from where Erin was standing. She looked back at Eli.

"Fine," he said.

He pulled back the hammer of his gun. Erin heard the click. She could see the black end of his barrel. And then, it all exploded. The last flash and crash Erin ever expected to hear.

He had shot her.

She flinched. Absorbing the fall. And the pain.

But it never came.

She opened her eyes. She wasn't hit. She looked at Eli. To understand. But he wasn't standing. Ben was yelling at her, through his taped mouth. His eyes were wide. He must have seen what she'd seen — Val's gun. And as Eli was pulling the trigger, Ben had thrown his weight into him. Knocking him off balance and causing him to miss Erin.

She dived for Val's gun on the floor. As she hit the ground, she grabbed it and smashed into Val's body in the process. But she was immediately on her knees. Without taking the time to stand up, she spun and pointed the gun at Eli.

But he was quick. He too was already back on Ben. Eli hit him in the face with the butt of his gun. Enough to hurt. But not enough to knock him down. He still needed his shield. Erin could see a line of blood above Ben's left eye.

Eli was looking at Erin now. "I'm getting tired of this," he said, in between breaths.

Erin assessed. They were back to where they were a moment ago. Ben was still Eli's hostage. And Eli still had a gun.

But now Erin did, too.

She held out Val's gun, using both hands, and pointed it at Eli's head.

Eli pushed his own gun farther into Ben's head, making him bend his neck to the side.

"Drop it," Eli said, slowly enunciating each word.

"No," Erin said.

"Work it out, kid." I shoot him. You shoot me. And you're left. All alone. With no one."

He was right. She shifted her feet. Val's gun heavy, holding it fully extended like this. Her odds *had* improved. She now had a gun. But Eli still had the upper hand.

Everything that's happened, she thought… and it comes down to this.

Erin lowed her gun, just a few inches.

"That's right," Eli said, softly.

Erin closed her eyes, and then opened them again. She looked at Ben. She thought she saw him nod. Whether she was waiting for that, or whether it just helped… she didn't know. But she was ready now. She aligned the sights on the front and back of Val's long handgun.

Taking aim.

And then, she pulled the trigger.

The sound, this close, would have been deafening. Much louder than the smaller gun Jonah had given her. And the kick would almost throw the gun out of her hand completely.

But she didn't notice any of that.

The only thing her mind could see, and feel, was Ben.

As he fell.

Her bullet had found him.

As she hoped.

She kept the gun high and fired, twice more. Willing them to take down Eli Bren. And they did. Everyone was down.

GONE

Erin dropped Val's gun and ran forward.

Eli had fallen off to the side and wasn't moving.

Erin slid down to a stop, next to Ben. The bullet had torn a hole in the side of his leg. She couldn't tell exactly where. Or even if it was still in there. She wasn't that good of a shot. And now there was so much blood. She was trying to put pressure in the right place. Ben's eyes were closing.

"Hang on, Ben," she said to him.

And then, at that moment, someone else was there.

Erin didn't hear him come up. And she didn't know he was there until she heard him say her name. She looked up. It was Gavin. He'd been here, in the Conservatory, the whole time — probably hiding, she thought. And she was thankful for that. He probably wouldn't still be alive if he *hadn't* been hiding. She wanted to thank him for the timely diversion earlier. But there would be time for that later.

"Get something," she yelled at him. "We need to stop the bleeding."

Gavin was looking around.

"My jacket," she said, pointing behind her. She'd taken it off earlier.

Gavin ran for it. In a second he was back, pushing it down into her hands. She took it, and pulled it under Ben's leg, wrapping it tightly, using her jacket's arms like a tie to make a tourniquet. Ben groaned.

"Hang on," she whispered to Ben again as she moved. She looked down at her work. It was tight. But she still couldn't tell if the bleeding had stopped. Her jacket was soaked in blood now. Gavin was still there, watching it all.

Then Erin looked up, remembering something else. Hale. He was still off to the side, unconscious, where he'd been the whole time. Hale had been beaten up pretty badly by Val. And he hadn't moved since everything had started. "Gavin," she said. "Check on Tom."

Gavin ran to him and kneeled down, looked at him.

"Check his pulse," Erin said.

Gavin reached under his jaw, and left two fingers there for a few seconds.

He looked up at Erin, nodding. "Yes," he said to her. "He's still got a pulse."

Erin let out a breath of relief and looked back down at Ben's leg. She'd hoped her jacket-tourniquet was working. But she still wasn't sure. Ben, for his part, had his eyes closed. She leaned close to him again. "Ben," she whispered.

He made a humming noise, but he didn't open his eyes.

"Ben," she said again, a little bit louder. "Stay awake. Stay with me."

He opened his eyes a little bit. She could hear him breathing. It was heavy. "I'm fine," he said. "Fine. Just… down here regrouping for a minute." He tried to smile, but stopped as it turned into a groan and a cough.

She put her hand on his forehead. He was hot. They

would need to get him to a hospital. Soon. She stood up, but then something stopped.

"Erin," Gavin whispered.

She looked at him.

"Look," he hissed.

Erin looked to where Gavin was pointing. A red spot on the floor. And next to it were a series of streaks. Erin stood up and then immediately started looking around.

"What is it—" Ben said, barely opening his eyes.

"Shh," she said to him. "Nothing."

But it wasn't nothing.

She was still turning, scanning the room.

The streaks of blood led off to the side. She knew she'd hit Eli earlier. It was a direct hit. She knew that. She *saw* it. But now... he was gone.

The red marks led out, back down the path she'd come in. She ran after it. The marks were getting lighter. But even in the low light of the Conservatory, she could still see a path of drips. She followed the trail. It led to an exterior door, and then disappeared outside. She looked around and swore. There was no more trail.

She ran back to where Ben and Gavin were.

Gavin was standing frozen, watching her.

"He's gone," she said.

65

ONE LAST THING

"GONE?" GAVIN SAID.

Ben moved on the ground. Erin sat back down with him.

"He was hit," she said. "And pretty badly, too."

Gavin was watching her. "Where did he go?" he said.

"I don't know," Erin said. "But if he was hit, then…," she stopped talking and looked up. There were red and blue lights reflecting through the domed glass ceiling above. She looked at Gavin and then back at Ben.

Ben's eyes were open, and he'd seen the lights, too. "They probably heard the gunshots," he said.

Over, off to the side, Hale was beginning to wake up. "Gavin," Erin said, motioning to Hale. He went to him, to help him sit up.

Erin looked around the room. The place was a mess. The trails of blood from Eli. The tall Christmas display Gavin had knocked down earlier. Making a timely diversion. It had cracked and was on the floor on its side. And then there was Val and Jonah, both laying motionless. Erin stood and walked to them. Val's body was laying on her side, her legs

still partially underneath Jonah's body. She bent down next to
Jonah. His body was at an odd angle. Erin reached to
straighten him some. She knew it didn't matter. But she did
it out of respect. Whatever of that there was left. She reached
down, moving his arms, putting them next to him. And as
she did, something small and dark slid out of his jacket
pocket.

She picked it up.

It was her audio recorder.

Back when all of this was starting, she'd been fidgeting
with it in her pocket. Eli and Val's eyes were on her, so she
couldn't pull it out and turn it on properly. And… at the
time, she wasn't sure if she'd actually managed to get it on.
Then, when Jonah frisked her in front of Eli and Val, he'd
slipped it out of her pocket. But he didn't hold it out, like he
did the gun, he quietly slipped it into his own pocket.

In everything that had happened tonight, she had
completely forgotten about it.

But now, holding it in her hand, she turned it over. And
the battery light was on. Her heartbeat picked up. This thing
was notorious for eating batteries. And she'd just changed
them before she'd come. If the battery light was on already,
that would mean it had been recording the entire time.

She quickly hit stop, followed by the rewind button,
pressing it a few times. It skipped back in thirty-second
bursts. She pushed play and held the tiny speaker to her ear.
She could hear sounds.

It had recorded.

It had recorded everything.

Erin turned and looked at Ben, holding up the recorder,
to show him. She was smiling. But…not because she was
happy. She wasn't. There had been too much carnage, too
much loss to feel happy. But still, she was smiling as she

looked at him. Maybe, just now, because of this, it was all over. And properly.

Ben was looking back at her. He didn't smile. She figured he was doing his best to stay awake. He'd lost a lot of blood. But he did see the recorder. He nodded, slowly. He understood. Erin turned and looked back at Jonah, at his face. His eyes were closed. She thought about what he had been when she met him. The man she knew him to be. And then, everything she'd learned in the meantime. About Lillian Lennox, his mother. And about how Eli had discarded her when she needed him most. And then, as a kid, living through that, watching it all happen. She knew… that kind of thing changes you. Whether you want it to or not. It just does.

And now, as she looked at him, still and not moving, he may have been the only person who really understood her. What she'd come through.

A warm little line ran down her face. She put her hand out and held onto his. She squeezed it. But of course it didn't respond. She put his back and slowly stood up.

Still looking down at Jonah when she heard footsteps, running into the large room. It was two police officers. They had their guns drawn. And they were about to tell them all to put their hands up, when they stopped, looking at the scene.

"There are four of us left," Erin said to the officers. "Two dead. And one escaped."

She slipped the recorder into her pocket and then lifted her hands.

"You," one of the officers said, looking at her. "Stay where you are."

She'd shown no signs of moving, or doing anything. But she knew was he just doing his job. And that was okay.

She inhaled deeply, smoothly, still keeping her hands in the air. The officers began to cautiously walk into the room.

As they made their way in, she let out the breath she was holding, the air flowing out calmly through her nose.

It was okay.

She was okay with everything now.

●66

THREE WEEKS LATER

ERIN CLOSED THE LID TO HER LAPTOP. SHE RUBBED HER eyes.

"Hey."

She jumped, not hearing him walk up. She turned around. Ben was standing in the doorway. "I didn't hear you come back," she said. She did most of her writing at a small desk in her bedroom. Her office had been converted to Ben's room, while he figured out what was next.

"I've been here for like an hour," he said, smiling.

"Oh," she said, rubbing her temples. "I think I need a break."

"How far in are you?"

She turned back to her laptop and was about to open it, to check, when she gave up midway through the motion. "I don't know," she said. "Maybe a third."

"That's good," Ben said.

"It started going a lot faster once they found Eli." On a yacht, off the coast of Mexico. Probably figured he was in international waters. It was the gunshot wound. That, and the blood he'd left on the floor in the Conservatory, were too much to overcome. Shortly after, the feds brought him in — Hale wasn't well enough yet to run point on that, but he still played a role in capturing Eli. It would all go in the book. Well, all but the part about Gavin. Somehow his involvement in all of this had leaked to the right circles and he'd been staying busy. It was nothing illegal, he told her, but it was the kind of work that was better left under the radar. So, for an old friend, she told him she'd keep his name out of the book.

And the book, she thought, rubbing her eyes again… All things being equal, it had a ridiculously tight deadline. But Erin understood. Strike while the iron is hot and all of that. And speaking of irons, *she* hadn't stopped getting calls and emails since this whole thing broke. But she'd largely ignored them. Except for the book, she was giving McGillis and the *Post* exclusive access. He was the one who got this whole thing rolling. The recordings she'd made weren't admissible in court, because D.C. requires two-side consent. Eli would have to have given his permission to be recorded. But they were certainly admissible in the media. And they'd set off a firestorm. One that ultimately — along with Hale's help — pressured the F.B.I. to re-route their investigation from Erin to Eli.

"Let's go downstairs," Ben said. "Take a break."

Erin nodded and stood up. She stopped, waiting on him.

"You first," he said. "The leg's still, you know, a bit slow."

Erin still felt bad about that. The surgery had gone well. And it didn't look like he was going to need any follow-up operations. Though, it was still a bit early to know for sure. He must have read the look on her face.

He pointed at her. "If I hear 'I'm sorry' once more," he said. "Then I'm going to shoot *you* in the leg."

She smiled. "Fair enough," she said. And the two of them walked downstairs. She went slow enough, to not leave him behind. At the bottom, Erin turned to walk into the living room. But Ben stopped in the foyer.

"Hey, uh, Erin?" he said.

She turned around. "Yeah?"

"I um," he said. "I was thinking… I mean, eh—"

"Ben," she said. "What."

"You want to go out later?" He spit the words out, probably less graceful than he'd intended. "Tonight," he added.

"Out?" she said, thinking about it. She'd been clocking a lot of hours on the book manuscript. And she knew taking a break would do her good. She nodded her head. "Yeah, sure."

"No," he said. "I mean, do you want to go out — with me."

"Of course," she said. "Who else would I…" And then, all at once, she understood what he was trying to say. As if he'd said a bunch more. It was like she just realized they were having a totally different conversion. And then she saw it. Ben, eternally comfortable in his own skin, was now, all of a sudden… nervous. She *had* been working too hard.

"Oh," she said.

"I mean," he added quickly. "We don't have to. If you don't want to, that is. I didn't mean to—"

"No," she said. "It's okay, I… I just…"

She looked at him again. All they'd been through together. She thought about it — all of it. What was his stake in all of this? Paul, sure. But there was a natural end to how far that would go. To how far Ben would need to take that. But, even before Paul died, Ben had come with her. Down to Colombia. But he didn't have to. He would never make a big deal of it — but he was talented. And well connected, too. He didn't *have* to hang around. In fact, doing so only hurt him, on a professional level. Turning down the new opportunities that came in, and all that.

She was looking at him, standing there.

"Okay," she said.

"Okay…?"

"Okay, let's do it," she said. "A date."

"Okay," Ben said, smiling.

Erin smiled back at him. She turned around, to walk into the living room. And as she did, she saw a tiny black and white picture on the narrow table in the foyer, next to where she normally dropped her keys. She'd seen it a thousand times. It was the best picture she had of her mother. Someone had snapped it, casually, when she was out on assignment somewhere. And it had found its way back to Erin. When she was a kid, she held on to it, and would sometimes sleep with it. But as she got older, she noticed it less often. Not that she didn't like it anymore. It was just one of those things, when we see something over and over, after a while, we learn to overlook it.

But now, still smiling, she saw it like she hadn't seen it in a long time. It was almost as if something about it was different. But she knew it wasn't the picture. It was something about *her* that was different. With everything she'd done, she could never bring her mother back. She knew that. She'd always known that. And, in fact, she couldn't reverse a single event. But… still. She'd done the right thing. And that mattered. She could feel it — it *did* make a difference. Inside of her, after all that had happened, something really was different now.

She looked back at Ben.

He was watching her, as she looked at the picture.

She smiled at him. "You ready?"

"What, now?"

"Why not?"

He shrugged. "Why not."

They grabbed their jackets from the rack in the corner. He opened the door for her. She walked out first and he closed it behind them. It was cold. The wind was sharp. But the sun was out, too. She waited for him, and then walked down, he following after her. With the two of them there, she decided to get a car. She'd been putting it off for years. But now, it felt right.

"Oh, and Ben?" she said.

He was still holding the keys in his hand. "Huh?"

"I do have one rule."

"Okay…" He stopped and looked at her.

She reached down and took the keys out of his hand. And then, holding them up, she said, "I drive."

He laughed. "You know, I remember your driving from Colombia."

They walked to the car. She looked at him, across the roof, and smiled as she opened her door. "Don't worry. I've gotten *so* much better since then."

THE TRINIDAD MAN

Thank you so much for reading the Erin Reed Trilogy!

And I know you don't want you to miss anything. Have you read *The Trinidad Man?*

It's the prequel to the series, set ten years before. Erin is just out of school, and the story explains why Erin left journalism in the first place. Oh, and it's <u>only</u> available at AJFontenot.com/trinidad.

P.S.

If you liked *The Vesper File*, would you please leave a **review** for it, wherever you bought it? That's huge. Thanks! - Joe.

ACKNOWLEDGMENTS

To Stacey (Mom), Marilyn Stewart, and Joe Waller, you were invaluable in helping me work through plot and structure. And, of course, to Kristin, for always keeping me from saying dumb things.

Thanks to Elena at L1graphics for making another cover that makes me want to pick up my own book and read it.

Thanks to my early readers — my BETA team, for your feedback; and my ARC team, for your honest reviews.

I am truly grateful for you all.

Want to connect? Find me online at AJfontenot.com. Or on Twitter @aJoeFontenot.